The Magnificent Mulligans™

BOOK FOUR

WHAT A CROC!

Bill Myers

Illustrations by Greg Hardin

FOCUS
ON
THE FAMILY.

*A Focus on the Family resource
published by Tyndale House Publishers*

For Natalie: Welcome to the family!

—B.M.

And we know that for those who love God all things work together for good, for those who are called according to his purpose.

ROMANS 8:28

Table of Contents

1
Just for Starters

"AUGH!"

In case you're wondering, that's the sound a chimpanzee makes when she's being attacked by a monster. (Especially a furry monster with a tiny head and humongous—and I do mean *humongous*—feet and a big tummy.)

"Winona, relax."

I spun around and saw my best pal, Stephie, trying to calm me. So I gave my standard

whimper, whimper, whimper
(This is the sound I make whenever I want attention—
which means I make it all the time.)

"It's just a mirror, silly," Stephie said.

I turned back to the monster and made a face. Its little pinhead made the same face back at me.

I waved my arms. The monster waved its arms.

I jumped up and down, and the monster . . . well, you probably get the picture.

Yes, I know it's just a reflection. But this reflection made no sense. How could my head have gotten so *tiny*? How could my great intelligence fit into such a little space? And how did my tummy get so *big*? True, I may have eaten a couple more hot dogs than I should have. (Okay, three or four more.) And little Julie hadn't missed the bag of peanuts I ~~stole~~ borrowed from her when we were on the Ferris wheel. But to have gotten so fat so fast?

No. Stephie was wrong. It *was* a monster. Just one that was good at playing ~~Monkey~~ *Chimpanzee See,* ~~Monkey~~ *Chimpanzee Do*.

"Turn around," Stephie said.

I wasn't crazy about turning my back on the creature, but I trusted Stephie, and . . .

There was another one behind me! (Sorry, I didn't mean to yell.)

Only this one had a giant head and a tiny body.

I looked up to Stephie, more confused than ever. It takes a lot of confusion to confuse my confusion with more confusion than my normal *confused* confusion is when it's confused.

Confused?

Me, too.

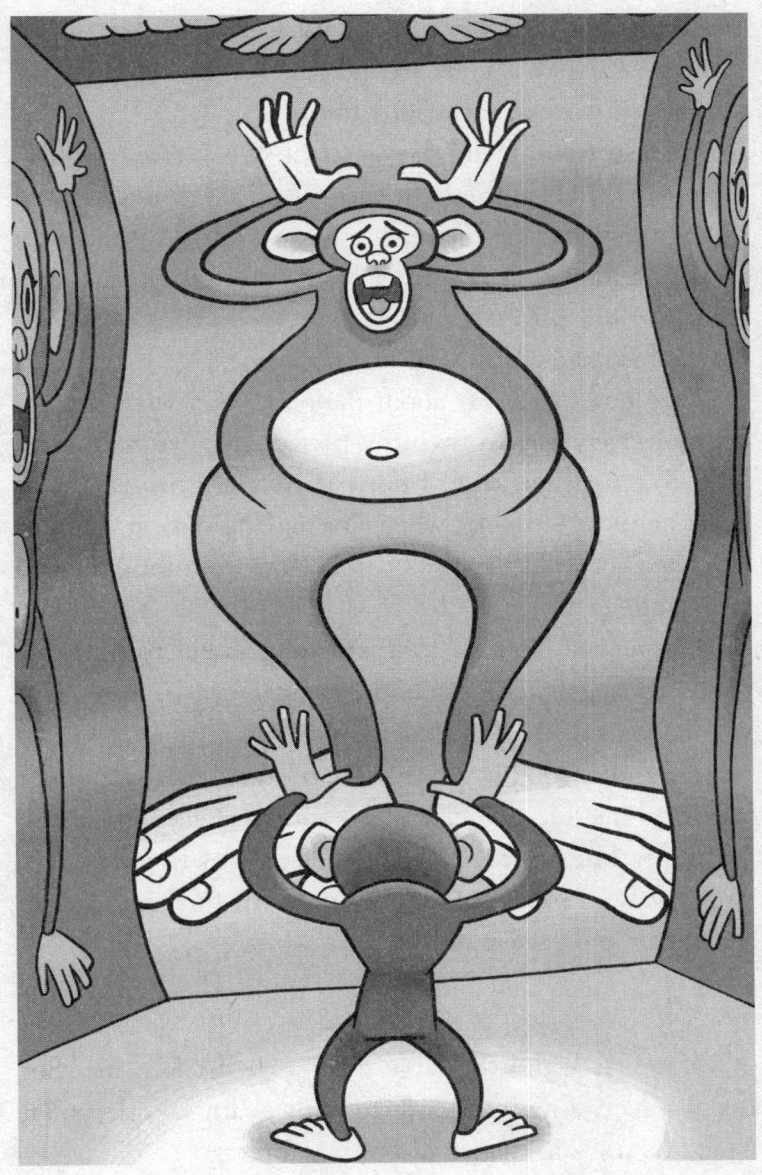

At least now you know how I was feeling.

Stephie giggled. "Look around you, Winona. All the mirrors are made weird so we look funny."

I looked around, and she was right. We were surrounded by mirrors. Lots and lots of them. And every one showed weird, creepy reflections of us. I frowned. Why did they charge us money to go into a room where they can't even afford *normal* mirrors?

Stephie laughed. "It's called a *fun house*."

I saw nothing funny about the place. Not when I go to the gym every day to keep my perfect chimpanzee figure. Actually, that's not true. I don't go to the gym . . . but I think about it—usually when I'm pigging out on a tub of ice cream (or whatever else I can borrow from the Mulligan refrigerator).

"Come on," Stephie said, reaching down to grab my hand. "Let's go back to the others and see if that attendant will let you ride the roller coaster now."

It sounded good to me. Earlier, the attendant would not let me on the ride—some excuse about me being an animal. (Honestly, humans can be so prejudiced sometimes.)

Anyways, I stuck my tongue out at the furry monster in the mirror and gave it a little

Pfftttt . . .

Of course it did the same thing right back at me. But that was okay. I was going off to another carnival ride, and it would be stuck in that stupid mirror forever.

2

The Race for Mayor

WHILE HALF OF US MULLIGANS were visiting the traveling carnival—eating, going on rides, eating, playing games, and did I mention eating?—Mom, Dad, Jessica, Lisa, and baby Al stayed at home. (Along with the 138 animals in our wild-animal park.)

Lisa, who is blind, wanted to get into the high school's marching band, so she was busy practicing her

Waugh-WAAAAUGH-WOOOOM

trombone (which actually sounds *worse* than what you just read . . . except to Buttercup, our elephant, who thought it was another elephant crying for help). Auditions were coming up for the marching band, and Lisa wanted to make sure she got in.

Jessica stayed behind to practice her cheer for the upcoming cheerleader tryouts (which also sounds worse than what you'll read now):

"Go, go! Get 'em, get 'em!
Bam! Bam!
Go, go! Get 'em, get 'em!
GooOOOOOO . . . CLAMS!"

In case you're wondering, our middle school's mascot is a clam. Don't laugh. It's better than the elementary school's mascot, which is a snail. Honestly, what cheer could possibly rhyme with *snail*? (*Stale*? *Fail*?) The poor mascot has to wear a giant plastic snail shell and crawl around on the floor.

Anyway, things at home should have been nice and peaceful, except that Lisa's and Jessica's rooms were right next to each other. This meant that Jessica could barely hear her own

"Go, go! Get 'em, get 'em!
Bam! Bam!"-s

over Lisa's

Waugh-WAAAAUGH-WOOOOM-ings

while Lisa could barely keep time to her music over Jessica's

"Go, go! Get 'em, get 'em!
GoooOOO . . . CLAMS!"

And since they both like to—how do I gently say this?—
defeat anybody and everybody they compete with (sorry, that's as
gentle as I can say it), they kept trying to drown each other
out until the whole house shook with

"Go, go!"
Waugh-WAAAAUGH-WOOOOM
"Get 'em, get 'em!"
Woom-WOOOOM
"Bam! Bam!"
WAAAUGH . . .
"CLAMS!"

Not a big problem, except that Mom and Dad were trying to watch Dad's television commercial about running for
mayor. That's right: Dad had finally decided to run against
Mayor Jowls.

"Girls!" Mom shouted. "*Girls!* Come on down and watch
Dad on TV!"

By the time they put away their weapons (their trombone
and pom-poms), the commercial was almost over. But not
before they heard Dad saying, "Even though Mayor Jowls is
a good guy, I hope you'll see that my plan is better."

When it ended, Lisa turned to Dad and asked, "That's it?"

Dad nodded. "Yep."

"But aren't you supposed to say mean things about the mayor?" Jessica asked. "So people will hate him and vote for you?"

Dad shook his head. "Mayor Jowls has his faults, but he still deserves my respect."

"But," Lisa protested, "that's not how you win elections."

"If that's what it takes to win," Dad said, "I'm not interested."

"But—" Jessica argued.

"But, but—" Lisa said.

"But, but, but—" Jessica added. (See what I mean about them being competitive?)

They would have gone on like that forever if Mayor Jowls's own commercial hadn't begun. I'll spare you all the boring political talk and cut to the chase, where he said, "My opponent, Michael Mulligan, knows nothing about nothing except that he wants to destroy our beloved city with his stupid wild-animal park. So vote for me, Mayor Jowls, and save our city!"

For a moment they all just stared at the screen.

Finally Mom shook her head. "Unbelievable," she said.

And for once in their lives, Jessica and Lisa agreed on something.

3
A Not-So-Good Idea

IT WAS A LITTLE EMBARRASSING being dressed up like a baby. The bottle Stephie gave me to suck on wasn't bad, but orange soda isn't exactly my favorite. (Why nobody makes peanut-flavored soft drinks is beyond me.)

But it didn't matter. Although the attendant let the rest of the Mulligan kids onto the carnival ride, he stopped me for the second time.

"Sorry, miss," he said to Stephie. "No children under four feet tall on the ride." As we turned to leave, he mumbled, "No matter how ugly they are."

I tried not to growl. (It's impolite for human babies to growl.)

But we weren't done yet. We came back again—only this time I was wearing my favorite disguise: a scarf, sunglasses, and a movie director's beret.

"Sorry," he said. "No, uh . . . um, what exactly are you?"

"You don't recognize her?" Nick asked.

The attendant frowned. "Um . . ."

Hector, our newest family member, asked, "You don't know the world-famous movie director, Suzy Speelberg?"

For the record, Hector wasn't *actually* lying; technically, he was just asking a question. And it might have worked if I didn't have this sudden urge to pick a flea out of my fur and eat it.

"Sorry, folks," the attendant said. "No flea-eating directors under four feet tall on the ride."

I wanted to check his rule book, but Nick said, "Let's just go. There are plenty of other attractions to see. Like that fortune teller over there." He pointed to a creepy-looking booth with all sorts of stars, cards, and wizards painted on it.

"It looks kind of scary," Janelle said.

"You're scared of everything," Nick said.

For once in his life, Nick was right. (Have I ever mentioned the time Janelle called 911 because she saw her shadow following her?)

"I don't know," Hector said. "In Colombia, we were taught never to mess with such things."

"Come on," Nick said. "Let's check it out. What can it hurt?" Before we could stop him, he started toward the booth.

And since he was the oldest, and since Mom said his job was to look after us (even though we all knew it should be the other way around), we followed.

Two minutes or three months later (chimps aren't great at telling time) we were sitting inside Madame Claire's fortune-telling booth. She had all sorts of crystal balls and burning candles. She also had a bowl of fortune cookies . . . which I quickly sat beside to guard. She wore long, flowing robes and had bright red hair, which would have looked more real if it didn't keep slipping down her head. She also spoke with a thick accent.

"I zee you have brought your pet monkey," she said.

I angrily answered, "OO-oo AH-ah EE-ee!"

"Vat iz she zaying?"

"She's a chimpanzee," Stephie said, "not a monkey."

I folded my arms and gave a stern nod.

Little Julie explained. "We own a wild-animal park just outside of town."

"I zee. And zo, you vant me to tell your fortune?"

Stephie piped up. "The Bible says telling fortunes is wrong."

"Ah, yes, zee Bible. It iz a cute little book, iz it not"—she squinted hard at Stephie and said her name—"Stephie."

Everyone froze.

"How . . ." Stephie swallowed. "How did you know my name?"

"I know many zecrets."

Maybe she did, maybe she didn't. The fact Stephie's name was stitched on the front of her coat might have helped. I would have pointed this out, but I was too busy guarding those fortune cookies.

Madame Claire forced a fake smile. "And zo," she said as she reached for her crystal ball and looked into it, "I shall now tell you . . . Vat!" she suddenly cried. "Oh! No! No, no, no!"

"Vat?" Nick said. "What is it?"

"Zee curse!"

"Curse?" Janelle asked.

"Zere iz a curse upon your family!"

We all traded alarmed looks.

"A curse?" Hector swallowed nervously. "What kind of curse?"

"Your land . . . it vas once an ancient burial ground. And zee spirits, zey are very, very angry with you."

"Angry?" little Julie squeaked.

"Angry?" Janelle repeated.

"What can we do?" Nick said.

"How can we make them happy?" Hector asked.

"It iz lucky for you, zat you haf come to me. I can remove zee curse, but only with zee help of thoze chicken featherz." She motioned to a shelf filled with plastic bags full of feathers. "Once you buy zee bag—I take Visa or Mastercard—I can reverze zee spell."

"That's all it takes?" Janelle asked.

"Zey are very special featherz."

"How much?" Nick asked.

"This veek ve haf a two-for-one zale."

"Terrific." Nick reached into his pocket.

"No, thank you," Stephie said.

We all turned to her and said, "*What?*" in perfect unison.

For a mini-human, Stephie could be tough. "We don't believe in curses," she said. "Even if we did, we don't need chicken feathers. We have God to protect us."

Nick shifted uncomfortably. "Well, yeah, um, there is that."

Madame Claire pushed up her wig. "Zo, you vill not buy my chicken featherz?"

Nick looked at Stephie, who frowned so hard that he shoved his money back into his pocket. "I'm zorry. Er . . . *sorry*," he said. "But my sister here . . . she's right."

"Vell zen, you haf my pity. Without zee featherz you vill have many, many problems. Ghozts, curses, you name it."

"Ghosts?" Hector tried swallowing but his swallower had run out of swallow.

"Iz a package deal," she said.

Nick took one more look at Stephie, then sighed and reluctantly rose to his feet. "We're sorry for wasting your time."

"Then move along." Suddenly Madame Claire's smile was gone. Come to think of it, so was her accent. "And make room for some paying customers."

We all traded looks.

"Go." Madame Claire pointed to the door. She raised her voice and called, "And my next client, you may reenter to conclude our biznezz."

We headed out the exit, but not before bumping into someone we never expected to see.

"Mayor Jowls!" Nick said.

The man looked at him. "You're one of the Mulligan brats."

"Yes, sir," Nick said. "What are you doing here?"

"I'm, uh . . ."

Before he answered, Madame Claire shouted at us, "I told you children to leave!"

"Yes, ma'am," Nick said.

We turned to step outside when she cried, "My fortune cookiez!"

We turned back.

"Zee zpirits, zey haf eaten all my fortune cookiez!"

We looked over to the bowl. She was right; it was completely empty.

"It iz a zign!" she shouted. "A zign zat you need my featherz!"

We all turned to Stephie, who folded her arms and shook her head. Of course she was right. Or was she? Maybe it really was a sign. At least that's what everyone thought . . . except for

BURP

me.

4

The Curse

MOOOOAANNNNNNN . . .

"Jessica?" Janelle whispered. "You awake?"

Nothing.

"Jessica?"

More of nothing.

Janelle jabbed her fingers into her twin sister's side. "Jessica, are you awake now?"

Reluctantly, Jessica stopped dreaming about winning the Cheerleader's World Series Superbowl. (As a jock, she sometimes mixed her interests together.)

"Do you hear that?" Janelle whispered.

mooOOaan**nnn**nnn . . .

"It's just Golda growling," Jessica said. She turned over and went back to winning the Gold Medal Stanley Cup Cheering event.

"Lions don't sound like that," Janelle said.

Suddenly a light shot across the window and was gone.

"Jessica!" More rib digging. "It's a ghost!"

That got her attention. So did the

mooOOaann𝗻𝗻𝗻ₙₙₙ...

Jessica threw off her covers and stumbled out of bed for the baseball bat beside the door. She had her doubts about ghosts, but if it was a robber, she'd at least welcome him with a nice headache.

The only problem was that Jessica was a major slob, which meant the floor was covered with

"Ow!"

trip-thud

football gear (complete with pads and helmet). After scrambling back to her feet, there was

"Ouch!"

stagger, stagger, stagger

the golf club bag (complete with clubs and balls). And finally there was

"Augh!"

tangle, tangle, tangle

the ice hockey goal (complete with steel frame and net).

Once Janelle untangled her, they raced into the hall and ran into . . .

"Ahh!" Nick and Hector yelled.

"Ahh!" Jessica and Janelle yelled back.

"What are you doing up?" Nick shouted.

"What are you?" Janelle shouted back.

mooOOaan**nnn**nnn . . .

With all the shouting (and haunting), Lisa threw open her bedroom door to join the party. Across the hall, so did little Julie and Stephie . . . with, of course, yours truly. (Normally Mom doesn't let me sleep with Stephie, but my newest disguise—Spider-Man pajamas with a Batman mask—threw her off.)

"Did you hear the ghost?" little Julie cried.

"It's the curse!" Janelle yelled.

Stephie argued, "There are no such things as ghosts and curs—" Before she finished there was another

mooOOaan**nnn**nnn . . .

and a flicker of light shooting across the window in the hallway.

"If that's not a ghost, it's doing a good imitation of one," Janelle said.

Stephie started down the hallway.

"Where you going?" little Julie cried.

"To get Mom and Dad."

It seemed a pretty good idea, and we all followed. But when Stephie arrived and knocked on their door, no one answered.

"Mom?" she said and knocked again. "Dad?"

Still no one.

The reason was simple. When we pushed open the door, neither one of them was there.

"Where are they?" Hector said.

"Do ghosts eat people?" little Julie asked.

"Don't be silly," Janelle said. "Ghosts don't eat people." She turned to Lisa. "Do they?"

Nick's cell phone rang, and he picked up. "Hello?"

We all waited. I took Stephie's hand. I knew she needed someone strong and courageous to comfort her. I also knew it was the only way to stop from passing out. It's not that I was scared. It's just that morning would be coming soon, and I've always hated missing breakfast before I die.

"Right," Nick finally said. "I'm on my way." He hung up and shoved the phone into his pocket. "Something is wrong," he said to us. "Mom and Dad need me down at the crocodile habitat."

"You're going outside?" Jessica asked.

"In the dark?" Janelle asked.

"All by yourself?" little Julie squeaked.

Nick took a deep breath and nodded.

"I'm going with you," Lisa said.

"No, Lisa. You look after the . . . womenfolk." Nick sounded very grown up. Or at least he tried to. "This is a job for me and Hector."

"Me?" Hector's voice quavered, sounding anything but grown up. "Why me?"

Nick set his hand on Hector's shoulder. "Because, amigo, every hero needs a sidekick."

"But—"

"And when it comes to saving this family, who is better than us?"

Hector turned to the rest of us. He obviously had lots of better choices in mind (which explains why I hid behind Stephie). But Nick had already started down the hall. And sounding like the superhero he always thought he was, he shouted, "Let's do this thing!"

With a heavy sigh, Hector followed. "All right," he said, "but if we die, you're going to live to regret it."

5
The Curse Grows

AT BREAKFAST THE FOLLOWING MORNING, everyone seemed a little nervous. Actually a lot nervous. And it wasn't just because it was Janelle's day to cook.

"Where's Mom?" Stephie asked.

"She's upstairs taking care of baby Al," Janelle said.

"Is he sick?"

Janelle nodded. "Running a low fever."

Stephie frowned. "What?"

Little Julie lowered her voice. "Baby Al getting sick. You don't think it's because of . . ." She lowered her voice even further. *"The curse?"*

"I thought we all agreed there's no such thing as a curse,"

Jessica called from where she was making six sack lunches for the kids. (Well, seven, if my newest disguise of skirt, blouse, and hair ribbon worked.)

Janelle crossed to the table with the tater tots she'd been making for breakfast. "Who's hungry?" she asked.

Of course we all were, until she started dishing them out. Instead of tater tots, they looked more like overcooked marbles. It didn't help that when she dropped them onto our plates, they *bounced* like overcooked marbles. And don't even get me started on how

"BLAH!"
choke . . . choke

they tasted.

"Winona?" Lisa said. "Are you at the table again?"

I told her *no* with my usual, "OO-oo AH-ah EE-ee."

But somehow, even though she was blind, Lisa knew it was me. "Sorry, girl," she said. "You know what Mom says about animals at the table."

Of course I knew, but that applied to *animals*.

Lisa grew sterner. "Winona . . ."

With a heavy sigh, I slipped off the chair and waddled for the door.

"And Julie," Lisa said, "that goes for the cockroach cage you're holding on your lap." (Lisa may be blind, but she is good.)

"It's for show-and-tell," Julie complained.

"Take it outside."

"Oh, all right," she sighed. But before she left the room with me, Nick bounded down the stairs to join everyone.

Normally he'd be in the bathroom fixing his hair for two or three weeks (or hours—you know how bad I am with time). But this morning he came down early to eat breakfast with us (or play marbles with the tater tots).

"So . . ." we all said nervously.

"So what?" he said.

"Last night!" We weren't exactly shouting but doing a pretty good job of talking at the top of our lungs.

Nick looked over to Hector. "Didn't you tell them?"

Hector would have answered, but he was still staring in shock at the marbles on his plate.

"Well . . ." Nick gave a hearty yawn. He loved telling stories, particularly when he was the hero. "By the time me and Hector joined Mom and Dad at the crocodile habitat, I'd already scared them off."

"You can scare ghosts?" little Julie asked.

"Have you seen his face?" Jessica said.

"Very funny," he said. "The point is I probably saved Mom's and Dad's lives."

We all knew that wasn't true. But since Nick is a legend in his own mind, we let it go.

"What about those lights?" Stephie asked.

"And all that moaning and growling?" little Julie added.

"I can't tell you about the lights. Like I said, they took off before I saw them. But Dad said moaning and growling are sounds crocodiles can make when they're upset."

"Or seeking a mate," Lisa added.

(See how educational these books are?)

"So that sound came from Samantha the crocodile?" Jessica asked.

"Except . . ." Nick paused to build suspense.

"EXCEPT WHAT!" everyone said. (Actually, this time we did shout.)

He answered, "Except . . . Samantha was nowhere to be found."

"Someone left the gate open?" Lisa said.

Nick shook his head. "Nope. It was closed. Sealed shut."

Hector added, "We checked all the fences, too. Everything was good."

"So . . ." Lisa said, waiting for more.

Nick shrugged. "So, Samantha just disappeared. Vanished into thin air."

Everyone got quiet . . . but we were all thinking the same thing.

Little Julie was the first to whisper it: *"The curse . . ."*

Suddenly the door flew open and we all kinda

"AUGH!"-ed

The good news was it was only Dad. The bad news was he said, "I can't take you to school today. You'll have to catch the bus."

"But it's raining," Janelle complained. "We'll have to wait in the rain."

Stephie joined in, "And get . . . wet!"

Dad chuckled. "You won't melt, Steph."

"What happened?" Jessica asked.

"It's the weirdest thing," Dad said. "I just had the van in the shop, but now, for some unknown reason, it won't start."

Unfortunately we all knew the reason. It had to be the . . .

CURSE . . . urse . . . urse . . .

In case you're wondering, that's an echo like in scary movies. Only this was no scary movie, it was the real

THING . . . ing . . . ing . . .

6

. . . and Grows

IF YOU'VE EVER RIDDEN a roller coaster, you know a little bit of what it's like to ride our school bus. Except it's more crowded and the screaming is three times louder. Of course, I wasn't on board—bus drivers are as prejudiced against chimpanzees as carnival ride attendants—but Stephie filled me in.

For starters, as the Mulligan kids boarded the bus, there were the usual complaints shouted from the other kids:

"You're standing on my feet!"

"Your knee is in my back!"

"Mou're melbow is mim my mooth!" (Which is the sort of thing you shout when someone's elbow is in your mouth.)

There was also the minor problem of Nick forgetting to brush his teeth:

"Did something die?"

"Please breathe the other way!"

"You're melting my glasses!"

And let's not forget Lisa looking for a place to put her trombone case.

K-Thud

"Ow, that's my head!"

"Sorry."

K-Pow

"That's my chest."

"Sorry."

K-Smash

"Thawth's my mowf."

But the real problem came with little Julie's bug collection. There must have been a hundred of them when she was at the breakfast table. And because only a few of them looked appetizing—chimps are picky eaters—there were still more than ninety left when I

burp

handed the cage back to her as she climbed aboard the bus.

It took a while to find a seat. But the good news is that she finally found one at the very back.

The bad news is that so did Bruce—the school's gigantic football star who got on board right after her. Because just as he was sitting beside her, the bus swerved hard to the left,

. . . which meant Bruce mysteriously fell to the right

. . . which meant he didn't sit beside Julie and her plastic carrying cage, he sat

K-RUNCH

K-RACKKKK

shatter, shatter, shatter

on *top* of them.

"Oh, sorry, little girl," he said as he jumped up.

"That's all right," Julie said. "I'm okay."

Unfortunately you couldn't say the same for her bug cage,

. . . which lay in broken pieces all over the seat

. . . which meant the bugs were running all over the seat

. . . which meant nearby kids were shouting and screaming,

"AWKKK! They're crawling on my leg!"
"EEEKKK! They're crawling on my shirt!"
"YIKES! They're crawling on my head!"

. . . which meant the driver slammed on his brakes

. . . which meant the pieces of cage flew forward into the rest of the bus

. . . which meant the bugs flew forward into the rest of the bus

. . . which meant the entire bus began

AWKKK!-ing

EEEKKK!-ing

and

YIKES!-ing

"What happened!" they shouted. "What's going on!"

For the Mulligans on the bus, there was only one answer, which is why Janelle panicked and screamed, "It's the curse!"

The kids around her shouted, "Curse! What curse?"

"The curse on our family!"

7

Rumors Spread

UNFORTUNATELY, THE FUN and games didn't stop on the school bus. At noon, when Nick dug into his lunch sack, he discovered he had six sandwich bags full of carrot sticks. No sandwich? No chips? No cookies? Since Jessica had packed the lunches, was this her way of telling him he should lose weight? As he looked down at the rabbit food before him, he thought of the other answer. It had to be the

CURSE ... urse ... urse ...

Lisa didn't do much better. All she got was six slices of plain bread.

Meanwhile, over at the middle school, as Jessica and Janelle sat down to eat . . .

"What?" Jessica cried as she reached into her lunch sack and pulled out six slices of bread covered in mustard and mayonnaise.

Janelle reached into hers. "Gross!" she cried as she pulled out six slices of ham. "What did you do?" she demanded.

"I packed everything," Jessica said. "I just . . . forgot to divide it up because of all our talk about the

CURSE . . . urse . . . urse . . ."

Over at the elementary school, Hector pulled out six bags of corn chips. Not bad. Better than all those carrots.

But the one who really lucked out was Stephie when she pulled out six bags of cookies.

Hmm, she thought, *maybe curses aren't such a bad deal after all.*

It would have been nice if the problems had stopped then, but . . .

After the little incident on the bus, plus all the talk of vanishing crocodiles, word of the curse quickly spread. By noon everyone was making fun of the Mulligans. Take Stephie for instance, when she was eating all those cookies:

"Hey, Steph, where did your mother get those? At the *ghosty* store?"

"Hey, Steph, is that where she buys your *sham-boo*?"

"Hey, Steph, for dinner are you guys gonna eat *spook-ghetti*?"

At first she tried to laugh, but the more the kids teased, the harder and harder it got. Not only was everyone rude, they were just plain *boo-ring*. (Sorry, I couldn't resist.)

Then there was Hector in P.E. class. The rest of the guys were too cool to say they were scared. Still, no one wanted him on their side in dodgeball . . . just in case the curse spread.

"I don't want him," they said. "You take him."

"I don't want him, you take him."

"No, you."

"No, you."

"I'll give you my baseball card collection."

"I'll give you my bicycle."

"I'll do your homework for a week."

"I'll do your homework for a month."

"Even math?"

"Uh . . . yeah, sure, even math."

"Sold!"

And once they finally started playing, Hector was the first to

K-Bam

get hit and get

K-Bam, K-Bam

hit again. And

K-bam!
bam-bam-bam

hit again. Everyone wanted to keep him on the sidelines away from them. One person even kept shouting, "Go to the principal's office! Go to the principal's office!"

And since it was the P.E. teacher, Hector had no choice.

8
Lying Billboards

THINGS WEREN'T MUCH DIFFERENT for Mom and Dad. Baby Al's nose had not stopped running, and Mom, like all good moms, was worrying way too much over every sniffle. Which explains why Dad was driving us in the car to the doctor's as

. . . Mom sat in the back watching Al's every breath

. . . I sat beside Mom like any good watch~~dog~~ chimpanzee

. . . cute little Julie sat beside me racking up eight gazillion points on her computer game with its annoying

BLEEP . . . BLOP
BLURP-s

(and some silly electronic song that kept repeating over and over . . . and over some more).

Dad glanced into the rearview mirror and asked, "Everybody okay back there?"

Baby Al answered with his cute *coo*, his cute *gurgle*, and a microscopic sniff.

"Hurry, Michael," Mom cried. "Al is getting worse!"

Of course he wasn't getting worse, and I tried comforting her with my best "OO-oo AH-ah EE-ee," which was interrupted when little Julie shouted, "ALL RIGHT!" as

BLEEP . . . BLOP
BLURP

she scored her nine billionth point.

Mom looked out the window and actually stopped worrying for a grand total of 1.5 seconds. "Oh, look," she called to Dad. "Someone put up a billboard for you."

We all looked and, sure enough, there was a giant billboard on the side of the road that read:

VOTE
Michael Mulligan
FOR MAYOR

"I guess you're right," she said. "It does pay to be nice."

Dad smiled. When he was right, he was right. And just

between you and me, he's usually right (except when he doesn't let me chew on the TV remote).

"Oh, look," Mom said, "there's another one!"

It had the same style of letters except it only spelled three words:

If you want . . .

"And another!" Mom pointed ahead.

This one had four words. But they weren't exactly the ones we expected:

THE WORLD'S WORST CROOK!

"I can't believe it!" Mom cried. "Who would do such a thing?"

Of course we all knew the answer.

"Mayor Jowls!" cute little Julie said.

"But why?" Mom asked.

Dad sighed. "The poor man wants to win at any cost."

Mom was busy grinding her teeth and trying to talk at the same time. "Okay (*grind*), if that's how he wants to play (*grind, grind*), we'll play with something even meaner (*grind, grind, grind*)."

"Tracy . . ." Dad said (which is the name he uses for Mom because that's her name).

"We've got to respond to this. 'An eye for an eye and a tooth for a tooth.' Maybe that old saying had a point."

"Tracy . . ." Dad said again.

"Michael . . ." (which is the name she uses for Dad because that's his name).

"I agree it's often difficult to love our enemies," Dad said. "But if the whole world believed in 'an eye for an eye and a tooth for a tooth,' we'd all be blind and toothless."

"But," she argued, "we have to do *something*!"

"You're right," he said, "we do."

"Like what?" cute little Julie asked.

Dad glanced into the mirror and answered, "Mom knows."

Mom let out a heavy sigh and finally answered. "I suppose we should show love to him. And pray for him."

Dad nodded. When she was right, she was right.

9
Go Clams!

SINCE CHEERLEADER TRYOUTS were coming up, Coach Buffton agreed to stay after school and help the kids practice. And since Jessica didn't understand that cheerleading was as much about dance as it was strength, she needed all the help she could get.

First up was Chloe Richardson, the super-rich, all-school mean girl. She took her position in front of the others, then smiled her every-tooth-in-perfect-place smile.

"Ready?" Coach asked. She turned to Petey McNurdy, the sixth-grade AV geek, who would be videotaping the girls so they could study their moves later. He nodded.

Chloe flipped back her every-hair-in-perfect-place do and smiled. "Ready."

Petey pressed the Record button and Coach called out, "Begin."

Chloe started her routine—clapping, dancing, and cheering:

> "Go, go! Get 'em, get 'em!
> **Bam! Bam!**
> Go, go! Get 'em, get 'em!
> GoooOOOOOO ... CLAMS!"

She was incredible. (The fact that she was rich enough to have her own personal trainer certainly didn't hurt.)

Everyone cheered wildly. (Again, being so rich that everyone wanted to be her friend didn't hurt.)

"Thank you, Chloe," Coach Buffton said. "It pains me to say it, but that was . . . perfect."

"Thank you, Coach," Chloe giggled in glee. (Which meant everyone else giggled in glee.)

"Okay, Jessica," the coach called, "you're next."

Jessica rose and took her place.

"Good luck!" Chloe shouted. "I hope the curse doesn't get you." Of course, Chloe didn't care. She just wanted to mess with Jessica's mind. And sadly, that's what happened. In fact, all Jess could think about was:

- the curse of the fortune teller . . .
- the ghosts from last night . . .
- the disappearing crocodile . . .

Coach nodded to Petey, then shouted to Jessica, "Ready?" But Jessica didn't hear. Her mind was too busy racing with memories of:

- the van that wouldn't start . . .
- the cockroaches loose on the bus . . .
- the lunch of six bread slices smothered in mustard and mayo . . .

Coach Buffton repeated, "Jessica?" Then louder, "JESSICA!" Jess blinked and came to. "Oh, sorry, Coach."

"Are you ready?"

Jessica nodded.

"Okay then." Petey pressed Record and Coach shouted, "Begin!"

Jessica waved her arms and yelled at the top of her lungs:

"Go, go! Get 'em, get 'em!"

So far, so good . . . except for Chloe covering her ears and crying, "I should have brought ear plugs!" . . . and the Chloe clones covering their ears and crying, "We should have brought ear plugs!"

Next came the *Bam! Bam!*

It was a simple move. All Jess had to do was stomp her feet. But because her racing mind forgot that she wanted to be a cheerleader instead of an Olympic athlete, her *Bam! Bam!* became a

K-BAM!

K-BAM!

She stomped the floor so hard that the whole gym shook.

"It's an earthquake!" Chloe laughed.

"It's an earthquake!" her clones laughed.

But the shaking gym wasn't the problem. It was Jessica's left ankle that had just crumpled under all the pounding.

"Augh!"

she cried as she fell to the floor. "My ankle, my ankle!"

Coach Buffton raced to her side. The others gathered around as Jess tried to stand and walk. But the pain was just too great, and she kept falling.

"Easy, girl," Coach Buffton said. "You've got a bad sprain."

Jessica looked to her, worried. "Does that mean I can't try out?"

"I'm not sure," Coach said. "It looks pretty bad."

Jessica bit her lip and closed her eyes, refusing to cry—not so much over the pain as over the defeat.

Even Chloe felt bad . . . though it wasn't exactly the sympathy Jessica wanted to hear: "It's the curse, isn't it?" Chloe said. "You really should have bought those chicken feathers."

10

All Things Work Together

EVEN THOUGH IT WAS STILL Janelle's day to cook, Mom has this hard-and-fast rule:

Everyone eats dinner together

(except for certain chimpanzees who've run out of disguises and have to sit outside the open window waiting for Stephie to bring scraps).

And Mom never allowed excuses. Not even . . .
"I'm staying after school to work on a class project."
"I'm rounding up more cockroaches."
"I'm at the doctor's getting a vaccine against Janelle's
    cooking."

So there they were, sitting around the table as Janelle served what looked like long pieces of straw . . . that were impossible to cut with their knives (or chew with their teeth).

"Ow!" Stephie cried. "I just cut my mouth!"

"Ouch!" Lisa cried. "I just pierced my tongue!"

"Aurgh!" Hector cried. "I just broke a tooth!"

Dad turned to Janelle and asked as politely as possible, "What, um, what exactly are we eating, sweetheart?"

Janelle beamed. "Spaghetti!"

"Isn't spaghetti supposed to be soft?" Nick asked. "You know, like noodles?"

"It is if you boil it," Janelle said. "But I tried something different. I baked it until it was nice and hard."

"Well, you certainly succeeded," Mom said as she pulled out a piece stabbing her in the cheek.

Dad thought it best to change the subject. "So, how was everybody's day?"

"Awful!" Stephie cried.

"Worse than awful!" Hector agreed.

"Worse than this spaghetti," Nick said.

"And all because of that stupid curse," Jessica mumbled.

"Curse?" Mom asked.

"From that fortune teller's booth at the carnival," Stephie said.

Dad frowned. "You went to a fortune teller?"

Oops. Everyone stared at their plates.

"What does God think about fortune tellers and curses?" Mom asked.

Stephie answered, "We're not supposed to mess with that stuff."

"And you went to the booth anyway?" Mom asked.

More plate staring.

Dad cleared his throat. "Guys, I'm a bit disappointed. I thought you knew better. We don't believe in curses. We don't listen to fortune tellers."

"But what about the car?" Lisa said. "Or baby Al, or the bus, or the messed-up lunches, or—"

Dad held up his hand. "Well, yes, bad things do happen in life. And good things too. But as Christians, we have Jesus and His angels to help get us through it."

"Will He protect us from ghosts?" little Julie asked.

Mom reached out and took her hand. "Sweetheart, there are no such things as ghosts."

"Even if there were," Stephie said, "Jesus would protect us from them—right?"

"That's right," Mom said.

Dad added, "Sometimes people have more faith in superstitions than they do in God."

Mom agreed. "And that's where the problems start."

Jessica raised her leg to show everyone the ankle wrap on her foot. "Like being so nervous we make things happen on their own."

"Does it hurt?" Stephie asked.

"Only when I'm awake," Jessica said.

"Will you still be able to try out for cheerleader?" Stephie asked.

"Maybe with this wrap," Jessica said. "We'll see."

"What about all the other stuff?" Nick asked. "Like Samantha the crocodile disappearing, or those billboards calling you a crook?"

Dad answered, "Sometimes it's just mean people doing mean things."

"And," Mom added, "even if the devil attacks us, the Bible promises that all things work together for good for those who love God."

"I do love God," Lisa said. "And I try to study and follow the Bible."

Mom nodded. "Jesus said that those who love God will obey His teachings."

"I still don't see how *all* things work together for our good. Some things just seem plain bad," Lisa said.

"Yeah," Hector said, frowning. "I don't know how everything that's happened can be working for anyone's good."

Mom answered, "It's not our job to figure out the *how*, Hector. It's our job to trust God and thank Him."

"That doesn't mean we thank God *for* what's happening," Dad said. "It means we thank Him in the *middle* of what's happening."

"'Give thanks in all circumstances,'" Janelle quoted. "That's our memory verse in school."

Mom nodded.

"Even when we don't understand?" Jessica asked.

"*Especially* when we don't understand," Mom said.

"Does that mean we have to thank God for this food?" little Julie asked.

"I suppose we can thank Him for it," Nick said. "But we don't have to eat it."

"Amen," Dad said under his breath.

Even Janelle agreed. That's when her face brightened and she suddenly said, "Hey, we've got pizza in the freezer. Anybody want pizza instead?"

"AMEN!" everyone shouted.

Janelle rose and headed to the kitchen while the rest of the Mulligans smiled gratefully. It was true, at least for that moment, that all things were working together for good.

11
Ghost Hunting

EVEN THOUGH IT WAS LATE, Lisa was really

Waugh-**WAAAAUGH-WOOOOM . . .**

going at it.

Sadly, none of us had the heart to tell her that playing trombone may not be her thing. Not that Mom didn't try. She used all the loving stuff they teach you at Mom School. Things like:

"Sweetheart, have you thought of switching to the kazoo?"

"Sweetheart, how about a quieter hobby, like knitting?"

"Sweetheart, do you really want to make us all lose our
minds?"

But there's one thing you can say about Lisa: She's determined. Another word that comes to mind is *stubborn* . . . real

WAUGH-WAAAAUGH-WOOOOM

stubborn.

The only one that seemed to like her playing was Buttercup, our elephant. Every time Lisa let out a good

woom-woom-WAAAAUGH

Buttercup would answer with her own trumpeting, er, tromboning that sounded a lot like

atreee-WAA

Sometimes the two had real long conversations (while the rest of us tried not going crazy).

Dad thought Lisa's playing reminded Buttercup of elephants calling to each other in the African wild. The rest of us thought we should take up a collection and send her there. (Lisa, not Buttercup.)

But tonight, none of that bothered Nick and Hector. After dinner, they thought up a plan to capture the ghost. Well, actually, Nick thought up the plan. Hector was too busy trying to talk him out of it:

"Dad said there are no such things as ghosts," Hector said.

"You heard the fortune teller," Nick said.

"Yeah, right. Sure."

"You saw the lights."

"Okay."

"You saw our crocodile vanish into thin air."

"About that . . ." Hector said. "Why would ghosts make a crocodile vanish?"

"When we catch them, we'll ask."

Of course, Hector had a few other questions. Minor things like *How exactly do you catch a ghost?* But Nick was too busy packing his sleeping bag to be bothered with such details. "Do you have the stakes?" he asked. "And the garlic?"

"I thought those were for vampires," Hector said.

"Don't be ignorant. There are no such things as vampires."

"Right," Hector sighed, "what was I thinking?"

"Oh, and make sure you wear something warm," Nick said as he grabbed a flashlight. "It's going to be a long night."

"We're going to be outside all night?"

"Of course not," Nick said.

Hector gave another sigh, this one in relief. "Good."

"We're going to be up in the tree house all night. Come on," Nick said. "Let's go!"

Before heading out, they stopped by the kitchen for the garlic.

After checking the last cupboard, Hector finally said, "It looks like there's no garlic."

"Okay, grab the dill pickles," Nick said.

"You can't catch ghosts with dill pickles."

"Doesn't matter. You can't catch them with garlic, either."

Hector was about to give another sigh, but then figured it wouldn't help anything.

They opened the door and started down the porch steps when they suddenly heard a loud

K-rash!

followed by

tumble "OO-oo"
tumble "AH-ah"
tumble "EE-ee"

They spun around to see me lying at the bottom of the steps. (Sometimes chimps don't see so good in the dark—especially when wearing sunglasses to disguise themselves from ghosts.)

"What is Winona doing out?" Hector said.

Nick shrugged. "She must have heard us. Chimps have a great sense of hearing."

(We also have a great sense of smell—especially when it comes to dill pickles.)

"Well, come on, Winona," Nick said.

I scrambled to my feet and followed.

Slowly, we worked our way through the animal exhibits—past the camels, past the aardvarks, and past my favorite, the meerkats.

"OO-oo AH-ah EE-ee,"

I called out. (Translation: "Hey guys, what's up?")

The meerkats immediately rose on their hind legs, looking into the sky. (They really crack me up.) But we'd no sooner passed them before Hector pointed.

"Look," he cried. "It's the lights!"

And he was right. They were the same ghost lights we'd seen floating across the grounds the night before. Only now they hovered a hundred yards away, near the penguin exhibit.

"Let's get 'em!" Nick shouted as he took off running. It sounded like a good idea, and I did the same . . . only in the opposite direction. (No jar of dill pickles is worth dying for.)

Hector liked my idea and would have followed, but it's difficult to run for your life when an older brother has grabbed your belt and is dragging you to your death.

Actually, it didn't matter. As soon as they heard our commotion, the ghosts vanished. Completely *disappeared*. Just like that.

"Where'd they go?" Nick cried.

Hector volunteered, "Maybe it's past their bedtime?"

Of course, Nick had to investigate. But when he arrived, there was still no sign of them. Nothing. Except . . .

"Look!" Hector pointed toward the penguin exhibit.

"What?" Nick shouted as he spun his flashlight toward it.

Hector gulped. "The penguins. Gertrude and Goony. They're . . . gone!"

12
Rumors Grow

THE NEXT DAY AT SCHOOL, word of the ghosts quickly spread—mostly because of Nick.

"Yeah," he bragged during first period, "I scared 'em off real good."

"Yeah," he bragged during second period, "soon as they saw me, they vanished."

"Yeah," he bragged during lunch, "I scared 'em so bad you'd think *they* were the ones seeing ghosts."

(Don't blame me, that's Nick's joke, not mine.)

Yes sir, once again it was:

NICHOLAS MULLIGAN...
LEGEND IN HIS OWN MIND

Unfortunately the legend didn't exactly help the rest of us kids. Take Lisa, for example. Billy Egobrat, the snobby drum major from band (who seemed to believe his life's calling was to be a world dictator), caught up to her in the hallway.

"Hey, Lisa . . . Lisa!" he said.

She slowed to a stop. She didn't have to see that it was Billy talking. His very voice made her skin crawl . . . along with everybody else's.

"You're not still trying out for marching band, are you?" he asked.

"I've been practicing all week."

"Right, but—"

"You don't think I can play trombone because I'm a girl?"

"Well, there is that, but—"

"You don't think I can march in the band because I'm blind?"

"Another excellent point, but—"

"But what?"

He lowered his voice. "My family is going on vacation to Disney World."

"So?"

"So, I don't want to get attacked and eaten by any ghosts before then."

Lisa laughed. "Billy, ghosts don't eat people."

Relief flooded his voice. "They don't?"

"Of course not. They just kill them and steal their souls."

Lisa didn't believe that. She just wanted to hear Billy gasp and freak out (which he did a pretty good job of) before she turned and headed down the hall. "See you at the auditions . . . if you're still alive."

But it didn't stop at the high school. The rumors and fears continued circling through the middle school as well—where there were thoughtful people, like Chloe Richardson, who were always happy to help.

"Coach Buffton! Coach Buffton!" she cried as the girls suited up in the locker room for their last cheer practice before tomorrow's tryouts.

"What is it now, Chloe?" the coach sighed. Coach Buffton often sighed when Chloe spoke. I guess you could say it's because Chloe wasn't a fan of physical education. She always seemed to have an excuse for skipping P.E. class. Sometimes it was:

- She just couldn't risk breaking her fake nails
- She just couldn't ruin her daily pedicures
- The doctor's note said Chloe was allergic to anything involving sweat

But that never stopped Chloe from complaining. "I'm just saying . . . and I think I'm speaking for all of us girls . . ." She turned to her crowd of wannabes who were already nodding up and down like bobbleheads.

"Go ahead, Chloe," Coach said. "What is it?"

"Well, we're all just worried about poor Jessica, that's all."

Of course, Jess and Coach didn't buy it. There were only three things Chloe cared about:

Chloe

Chloe

You guessed it: Chloe

"Thanks," Jessica said. She'd just finished wrapping her sprained ankle. "With this bandage I'll be fine."

"I'm not talking about your ankle," Chloe said. "I'm talking about if you come to our games with that curse and those ghosts following you. I mean, how do you expect our team to ever win?"

"There are no such things as ghosts and curses," Jessica said. "That's just stuff we see in the movies."

Chloe put her hands on her hips. "Like all those bugs your sister let loose all over the bus?"

"That was an accident."

"Or your brother's talk about fighting off ghosts all night?"

"That's just Nick . . . being Nick."

"Or that crocodile that's running around in the showers behind you?"

"Don't be ridiculous," Jess said as she turned to the showers. "There's no—

AUGH!"

But Jessica wasn't the only one screaming. So were all the other

"AUGH! AUGH!"
"AUGH! AUGH!"

cheerleaders. Come to think of it, so was

"AUGHHH!"

Coach Buffton.

And *why* was everyone screaming? Well, because that's the thing you do when a live crocodile is thrashing around in the showers of your locker room!

13

A Special Guest Appearance

OF COURSE SAMANTHA, our crocodile, was disappointed the girls didn't stick around to play. Or at least share a nice meal (like a slower-running girl or two). Not that you could blame her. It had been two days since she'd eaten, and with so many bare feet running past her, she figured they wouldn't mind if a few tasty toes went missing.

But the girls had other ideas. Without even saying good-bye, they ran into the hallway, screaming their little bobble-heads off.

"WE'RE ALL GOING TO DIE!"

Talk about rude.

With no food in sight, Samantha followed them into the hallway. Sadly, the manners of those in the hallway were just as bad, especially with the youngest ones screaming, "STRANGER DANGER! STRANGER DANGER!" To make matters worse, they ran into their rooms and

SLAM SLAM SLAM-ed

their doors without ever once inviting her inside.

Only the science room was left open. No students had entered. In fact, the only living creatures inside were two little white mice in a cage on the table. Well, there *had* been two little white mice in a cage on the table. But with a flip of Samantha's powerful tail, the cage

Bam! Crash!

fell and opened. And those two cute little white mice? Well, let's just hope

squeak squeak
gulp gulp
BURP!

they had a nice life.

I'll save you the rest of the boring details. Little things like:

- the police department coming out
- the fire department coming out
- the TV news crew coming out

And let's not forget Mayor Jowls, who just loved seeing himself on the TV news.

Of course, Jessica called Mom and Dad. "Hurry," she cried, "get down here before these people do something crazy!"

Sadly, "crazy" was already happening . . . and it was only getting worse.

By the time Mom and Dad pulled up, Samantha was already outside the school and crawling toward the school's fountain. It was a round pool of water with what else but a giant concrete clam in the middle that was spitting out water. When Mom and Dad leaped from their van, the reporters swarmed all over them like fans at a Taylor Swift concert.

"Are you sure the alligator is yours?" they shouted.

"She's a crocodile!" Dad shouted.

"Aren't they the same?" they shouted.

"Not to them!" Mom shouted back.

Meanwhile, Samantha had crawled over the edge and splashed into the fountain.

"Okay," Dad yelled to Mom as they pulled a big cage out of the van. "Let's set this in the pool as close to Samantha as possible."

"Right," Mom shouted.

But even as they carried the cage, the reporters followed, never letting up.

"Why did you let your children bring it to school?"

"Don't you know how dangerous alligators are?"

"What if it eats one of the students?"

For a moment, Dad wondered if Samantha might actually prefer the taste of reporters, but he pushed the thought out of his mind. After all, reporters were people too. Most of them.

Not that it mattered. At the moment, Samantha was too busy trying to eat the giant concrete clam out in front of the school. (You may remember that the school mascot is a clam.)

Together, Mom and Dad eased the cage into the pool just a few feet from Samantha.

"Hey, girl," Dad called.

Still thrashing back and forth, Samantha turned from the clam.

"Careful, Michael," Mom warned.

Dad nodded. "Okay," he said, "hand me the chicken."

Mom reached into her bag and pulled out half of a frozen chicken (a crocodile's favorite snack). She handed it to him.

The reporters instantly demanded, "Why are you killing innocent chickens?"

"Does the Society for Prevention of Cruelty to Chickens know about this?"

Dad ignored them and carefully waved the chicken over Samantha's head so she could see and smell it.

Meanwhile, Mayor Jowls was getting jealous over all the attention he was *not* getting. So he leaped onto the edge of the fountain and shouted, "Look at this fool!" Pointing at

Dad, he yelled, "Is this the type of man you want to have as your next mayor?"

But no one listened. What Mom and Dad were doing was far more interesting. Once Dad had Samantha's attention, he tossed the chicken into the back of the cage. And since frozen chicken tastes better than concrete clam, Samantha scrambled after it, thrashing her tail all the way.

Mayor Jowls shouted even louder. "He's not a leader of men! He can't even—" The mayor would have continued his insults, but it's hard insulting people when a crocodile's tail slaps you off your feet and you

"AUGH!"

SPLASH!

fall into the water.

The good news was that Samantha was far more interested in raw chicken than shouting politicians. Once she was inside the cage, Dad quickly closed and locked it.

The bad news was . . . when the mayor came up from the water, gagging and gasping, he had lost his toupee.

But at least he got the attention he wanted. Not only did he make it onto the nightly news, but every paper in the county had a photo on their front pages of the bald, dripping-wet mayor coughing and sputtering out water . . . not that different from the clam.

14

Just Hanging Around

LATER, AFTER SCHOOL, Nick and Hector worked with Dad to set up lights around the park. I helped . . . until I discovered that electrical cables were even tastier than TV remotes.

When Dad saw me, he ordered, "Winona, go into the house with Stephie."

I would have protested but it's hard protesting with a mouthful of cable.

"Besides," he said, trying to make a joke, "biting into these wires could be a shocking experience."

I didn't laugh. (It's hard to laugh when you're sulking.) Instead, I let Stephie take me inside where I'd show my appreciation for his humor by doing a little extra TV-remote hunting.

Once they finished setting up lights around the sea otter exhibit, they grabbed the ladder and cables and headed over to where we keep Sally the gorilla.

"You really think these lights will work?" Nick asked.

Dad answered, "Hopefully they'll scare off whoever is stealing our animals."

"You still don't believe it's the curse?" Nick asked.

Dad shook his head. "Not for a second."

"Even if it's being helped by the ghosts?" Hector asked.

Dad shook his head. "Whatever is happening is being done by people."

Hector glanced nervously around. "By 'people,' are we talking . . . dead people?"

"Son," Dad said. "There are no such things as ghosts."

Usually we believe Dad, but with all that was happening, everyone started having their doubts.

When Dad and the boys arrived at the gorilla exhibit, Sally met them with her usual pacing and howling. I don't want to say she's a grump, but each year when the animals put on *The Grinch Who Stole Christmas*, she always plays the lead.

"Hector?" Dad pointed to a large, flat stone at the base of the exhibit. "Set the ladder there. Hold it steady, and I'll climb up and fasten the lights to that overhanging rock up there. And Nick," he said, "as I climb up, feed me the cable so I—"

"Let me do it," Nick said.

"Fasten the lights?" Dad asked.

"Absolutely," Nick said. "Nobody climbs ladders and

fastens lights as good as me." (We've already covered Nick's pride problem, right?)

"Well, okay," Dad said. "But be careful."

Nick threw all the cable over his shoulder and started up the ladder.

"Don't take it all," Dad said. "Let me feed you the cable as you need it—that way you won't get tangled up in it."

"No worries," Nick said as he continued to climb. "I can handle it."

Meanwhile, Sally, who did not appreciate people climbing above her home, began jumping up and down . . . while throwing in some extra

HOWL-ing

and

GROWL-ing

But Nick continued to the top of the ladder where he began hanging the lights. "Chill, banana breath!" he shouted down at her . . . which only made Sally

HOWL

and

GROWL

louder.

Nick laughed, barely noticing that he was getting tangled in the cable as he shouted at her. "I don't blame you! If I had your looks, I'd be howling too."

"Nick," Dad warned, "don't tease her."

Working, but getting even more tangled, he shouted, "Monkey mind doesn't mind!"

"Just attach the lights," Dad said.

"I don't know," Nick yelled, trying to untangle himself and leaning backward. "She'd be better off in the dark. I mean with a face like that . . ."

"AUGHhhh . . ."

Nick would have continued his insults but it's hard insulting gorillas when you're falling into their exhibit.

"Nick!" Dad shouted.

If she could, Sally would have grabbed him. Fortunately there wasn't enough extra cable for him to fall all the way to the ground. So instead of becoming Sally's afternoon snack, Nick hung upside down just inches out of her reach.

"Nick!" Hector yelled.

"Nicholas!" Dad cried as he raced for the ladder.

When Nick found his voice, it shook worse than Jell-O on a jackhammer in an earthquake. "I-I-I'm c-c-cool," he said.

Dad started climbing. "Just stay put! We'll get you down!"

"G-g-great!" Nick answered, hanging just feet above Sally's leaping, *HOWL*-ing, and **GROWL**-ing. "Oh, and Dad?"

"Yes, Son?"

"I'll need some dry underwear."

15

Late Night News

AFTER NICK GOT UNTANGLED (and found some dry underwear), we all had dinner. Well, not exactly *we*. The good news was, it was Mom's turn to cook. The bad news was, I was still out of disguises so she put me outside with "the rest of the animals."

Animals! Me?

(Sorry for yelling.)

But that didn't stop Nick from inviting all us kids (human and other) to spend the night in the tree house. The reason? To watch for ghosts.

Once we got there, we climbed the twenty-foot ladder, stepped inside, and waited. Everyone was there except:

- baby Al, who always slept through the good stuff (when he wasn't crying through it)
- cute little Julie, whose bedtime was so early she had to sleep through the good stuff
- Jessica, who was upstairs getting ready for tomorrow's cheerleading tryouts:

"Go, go! Get 'em, get 'em!
OW! OW!"

(That's the sound of a sprained ankle.)

- Lisa, who was still practicing her trombone:

Waugh-WAAAAUGH-WOOOOM . . .

(Which still sounds worse than it reads
. . . except to Buttercup.)

I tried to talk Stephie into staying behind—after all, us girls need our beauty sleep, not to mention late-night snacks—but she wanted to go. And since I'd die for my little friend (as long as it wasn't too dangerous), I tagged along.

Hector leaned against one side of the tree house. "You really think they're going to show?" he asked. "Now that we've got all the lights set up?"

Stephie added, "Aren't ghosts afraid of light?"

"We'll see," Nick answered as he carefully surveyed all the animal exhibits and habitats.

"If you ask me, the whole thing is stupid," Janelle said as she checked her cell phone. Janelle always checks her phone—at least when she's awake . . . and sometimes when she's asleep. (You've heard of sleepwalkers? Janelle is a sleeptexter.)

"Why do you think it's stupid?" Nick said.

"Because there are no such things as ghosts or curses or any of that."

Hector smirked. "Tell that to our crocodile."

"Samantha just wandered off," Janelle said.

"And magically appeared at our school?" Hector asked.

"And what about Gertrude and Goony?" Stephie said. "Did they just wander off too?"

Janelle would have kept arguing, but it's hard arguing when your mouth is hanging open at what you've just seen.

"Janelle?" Nick asked. "You all right?"

Instead of answering, she simply stared at her phone.

"Janelle?" Stephie asked. "What are you looking at?"

Ever so quietly, Janelle mumbled, "The news."

"Cool," Hector said. "Are they showing Mom and Dad rescuing Samantha?"

Nick smirked. "Let's hope they got a nice shot of Mayor Jowls spouting water."

Without a word, Janelle turned her phone and showed us. It was the news, all right. But instead of the mayor's video, it showed the two anchorpeople staring wide-eyed at the news desk directly in front of them.

The reason?

Gertrude and Goony were waddling across their desk!

Well, Gertrude was waddling.

Goony had stopped at the middle, thinking it might be a good place to poop.

"Goony!" Stephie yelled.

"No way can they be there!" Nick shouted. "The TV station is on the other end of town!"

Hector shook his head. "Goony never had any manners."

"No way could they have walked there!" Nick repeated.

Before any of us could answer, we had a couple more surprises. Little things like . . .

Surprise #1

A faint noise that sounded a lot like:

k-thud

Surprise #2

At that exact moment, half the lights in the park went out.

"What happened?" Stephie cried.

"What's going on?" Hector shouted.

Unfortunately no one had an answer. (Actually, we all did, but no one wanted to say it.) Instead, we shuffled to the edge of the tree house and looked out over the darkened half of the park.

Janelle cleared her throat and in her best grown-up voice said, "It's probably just a blown fuse."

Nick turned and started for the ladder.

"Where you going?" Hector asked.

"If it's a ghost," Nick said, "I'm going to stop it!"

We all traded looks. That's one thing you could say about

Nick: He was brave. (Another thing you could say about him: He wasn't always smart.)

"You're not climbing down there," Stephie said.

"Why not?" he asked.

We had hundreds of reasons (or maybe a thousand, since you know my math skills). But they all spelled the same thing:

D - E - T - H

(Sometimes I'm not so good at spelling, either.)

16
Stranger and Stranger

"YOU'RE NOT GOING BY YOURSELF!" Janelle said.

"Of course not," Nick said. He turned to Hector. "You're coming, right?"

Hector swallowed.

Nick repeated, "Right?"

More swallowing.

"I mean that's what sidekicks do . . . right?" Nick asked.

No one was sure when Hector signed up for that job, most of all Hector. But with all our eyes on him, and not wanting to be a chicken, Hector's voice squeaked out a "Yeah, sure" (though his expression screamed a "NO WAY!").

The two started down the ladder.

Janelle hesitated, then followed. "Well, I'm not staying up here with just Stephie," she said.

Stephie hesitated, then followed. "Well, I'm not staying up here with just Winona."

I hesitated, then followed. "OO-oo AH-ah EE-ee."

(Translation: "Well, I'm not staying up here with just me.")

Once we got to the ground, we turned on our phone lights. Except me. (Dad once gave me an old, hand-me-down cell phone until I discovered it tasted even better than the television remote.)

Nick took a deep breath. "All right," he said, "let's do this." He gave Hector a nod and they headed to the dark side of the park . . . while Janelle, Stephie, and I headed to the lit side.

When Janelle saw where the guys were going, she called out, "Why are you going that way?"

"That's where the ghosts will be," Nick said. "Why are you going that way?"

"That's where they won't be."

"Come on," Nick argued. "Either we're going to scare those things off or we're not."

Stephie chimed in, "I vote *not*."

"And what do we do then?" Nick asked. "Just let them keep sucking our animals into the multiverse or whatever they're doing?" He pointed at me. "Who knows, Winona could be next."

I clutched Stephie's hand. Not because I'm an animal but because without my disguises, the ghosts might mistake me for one.

"Look!" Hector pointed off into the darkness where a light floated in the air.

"Let's go!" Nick shouted and started running.

Unfortunately, it was toward the ghost and not away from it.

Unfortunatlier (one of my favorite made-up words), Hector followed.

Unfortunatliest, Janelle, who didn't want to be left alone, gave a sigh and followed.

Which meant Stephie gave a heavier sigh and followed.

Which meant I gave my heaviest *whimper whimper* as she dragged me along. (Holding Stephie's hand has its disadvantages.)

The light was at the far end of the park, so we had to run past a lot of the animal exhibits in the dark. If the animals didn't see us, they sure heard us. Which explains all the

GROWLING and BARKING

CHIRPING and *CAWING*

not to mention the

gurgle, gurgle, gurgl-ing

(Those sea otters, they're always fooling around.)

"We're almost there!" Nick yelled.

The good news was the ghosts never had a chance to get away.

The bad news was the ghosts never had a chance to get away.

But the closer we got, the less and less they looked like ghosts . . . unless ghosts disguise themselves as a flashlight tied to a tree branch waving in the wind.

"What's going on?" Nick asked as we arrived and stared up at the branch.

"I don't get it," Janelle said, leaning over and trying to catch her breath.

I would have agreed but it's hard agreeing when you're— *pant, pant, pant*—wheezing out a lung or two.

"Why would the ghosts bring us all the way out here?" Stephie said. "It makes no sense."

"Unless . . ." Hector looked back to the park.

"Unless what?" Nick said.

"Unless this was just a decoy to throw us off."

"Throw us off of what?" Janelle asked.

Hector pointed back to the lit area of the park. "Off of what they're really doing."

I turned and, sure enough, saw that there were more floating lights . . . way over by the seal exhibit.

"He's right!" Nick cried. "It's a trick!" He started running back across the park. "Come on!"

Everyone took off with him.

Well, everyone but me and Stephie. Poor thing. She tried her best to hide it, but she was way too exhausted to run. That's why I held her back, insisting we walk very, very slowly. But Stephie is stubborn . . . which explains why she

picked me up, threw me over her shoulder, and carried me.
(She can really put up a brave front.)

When we finally arrived, Stephie asked the others, "Where
are the ghosts, and where are the lights?"

"Gone," Hector said.

"Which?" Stephie asked. "The ghosts or the lights?"

"Yup," was all Nick said as he looked out into the night.

"Both of them?" Stephie asked.

"Not just them." Janelle motioned to the seal exhibit
beside us. Weird. Even with all the commotion, none of our
seals, Larry, Moe, and Curly, had come out to investigate.

"Where are they?" Stephie asked. "What happened to the
seals?"

"Yup," Nick repeated. "They're gone too."

17

A Breakfast Disaster

THE FOLLOWING DAY it was Nick's turn to cook . . . which meant cold cereal for breakfast. Nick really wasn't lazy, it's just . . . well, okay, he is a little lazy. But with all the time in front of the mirror getting his hair just right, he can't be expected to spend time creating gourmet meals.

This morning was no different. Well, maybe a little:

"Hey, Nick," Lisa said.

"Yeah?"

"You forgot the spoons."

"Oh, right." Nick raced back into the kitchen and grabbed the spoons. When he came out he tossed them

clang, clang
clatter, clatter, clatter

onto the table in front of us.

"Uh, Nick?" Mom said.

"Yeah?"

"You forgot the milk."

"Oh, right." He raced back into the kitchen, grabbed the milk, came out, and

glug, glug, glug, glug . . .

began pouring it absentmindedly into where our bowls should have been—if he'd not forgotten the bowls, too.

"NICK!" everybody shouted.

It was definitely not one of his better days.

Mom and Dad took it all in stride. They were used to minor (and in Nick's case, major) catastrophes.

After cleaning up the mess, we got down to eating, which involved a lot of

crunch, crunch, crunch-ing

since there was no milk left to pour on our cereal.

Hector turned to Dad. "Still no sign of the seals?" he asked.

Dad shook his head. "I called the police. Officer Tippet is looking into it."

"I didn't know Officer Tippet was a ghost expert," little Julie said.

"Julie," Mom said, "remember there are no such things as ghosts."

No one spoke a word, which is a lot like no one agreeing. Instead, everyone went back to their

crunch, crunch, crunch-ing

Finally Dad changed the subject. "So, Jessica, today is your big cheerleading tryout?"

She nodded.

"You sure you'll be okay with that ankle?" Mom asked.

"I'll be fine as long as I keep it wrapped," Jessica said.

"And the curse doesn't get you," Hector mumbled.

Dad shot him a look. Hector looked down.

"And Lisa," Dad said, "how's that trombone coming along?"

"I'm getting a lot better."

Dad tried his best to sound positive. "Really?"

"Can't you tell?" she asked.

"Um, er . . ." Dad looked at his cereal, and everyone returned to

crunch, crunch, crunch-ing

"Well," Mom spoke up, "Buttercup seems to like it. Every time you play, she's out in the habitat tooting and trumpeting back. It's so cute the way she answers."

Lisa sighed. "Things would be a lot easier if Billy Egobrat didn't hate me."

"Who?" Mom asked.

"He's the drum major."

"What's a drum major?" little Julie asked.

Lisa explained. "He's the guy who marches ahead of the band waving a baton around to direct everyone. And Mr. Crumpton, the band teacher, is letting him make the final decision about who gets into the marching band."

"Why doesn't Billy like you?" Mom asked.

"He says he's afraid of the curse, but I know the real reason."

"Which is?"

"He thinks I can't march with them just because I'm blind."

"You're sure that's his only reason?" Nick said.

"What else could it be? With as good as I play, it's his only excuse."

Everyone traded looks and went back to

crunch, crunch, crunch-ing

"So, how's the campaign coming along?" Nick asked Dad. "You've got a big debate tonight, right?"

A Breakfast Disaster

"Can we come to watch?" Stephie asked.

"Of course," Dad said.

"You're going to be mayor, aren't you, Daddy?" little Julie asked.

Mom and Dad glanced at each other. Finally, Mom answered, "Mayor Jowls has been saying a lot of mean things about your father. None of them true, of course, but—"

Julie jumped in. "But you're going to win anyway 'cause good guys always win, right?"

"Um . . ." Dad took another bite and

crunch, crunch, crunch-ed

"It just doesn't seem fair," Janelle said. "All this bad stuff happening to us."

"Sweetheart," Mom said, "God never promised us life would always be fair."

"But you said everything works together for good if we love God," Janelle said.

"That's right. But sometimes our version of *good* isn't as good as God's version."

"What do you mean?"

"I mean sometimes we don't understand what's happening. And sometimes it can really be confusing . . . at least for the moment."

Dad nodded and continued, "But if we stick with Him,

if we continue to love Him, even when it doesn't make sense, things eventually do work together for good."

"Always?" Stephie asked.

"What's the verse say?" Dad asked. "Romans 8:28."

Julie stopped crunching long enough to quote, "For those who love God all things work together for good."

"That's right," Mom said. "Not some things. Not most things. But . . ." She waited for Julie to answer.

"*All* things!" Julie exclaimed.

"That's right," Dad said. "All things."

Everyone looked around the table. I'm not sure they believed his words any more than they believed what Mom had said about ghosts. Either way, it didn't stop them from

crunch, crunch, crunch-ing . . .

18
Marching Orders

"ALL RIGHT, EVERYBODY!" Billy Egobrat stood in front of the band looking as proud as any future world dictator could look. They were out on the football field at noon, practicing one last time before he chose who would be in the marching band. "I want everyone in their positions, and I want them there this very instant!" (See what I mean about him being a dictator?)

Everyone scrambled to their assigned places . . . one row behind another, behind another, behind another. Lisa was no exception. She'd done her homework ahead of time. She knew exactly how many steps to take to get into her place. People often think that being blind is a big disadvantage. Lisa knows better. Sure, she has to work harder, but that harder work always makes her better.

"Wait a minute!" Sammy Dimberg shouted. "I'm lost."

"Me, too!" someone else yelled.

A third shouted, "I thought I was over here, but now . . . where am I?"

Soon everybody was wandering around the field like ants over a honey jar. You've never seen ants swarming over honey? Not a pretty sight . . . (unless you're a chimp who loves honey and doesn't mind a few dozen ants tickling your throat on the way down).

The point is, everyone was lost.

Well, almost everyone.

"Look over at Lisa," Sammy shouted. "She's standing in the right place."

Lisa raised her hand, and everybody raced to her and found their own places.

Of course Billy Egobrat pretended not to notice. "All right!" he shouted. "You will begin marching when I blow my whistle—one long and four short, like this." He put the whistle to his mouth, took a deep breath, and

TWEEEEEEET . . .
TWEET-*TWEET*-TWEET-TWEET

(I don't want to say he sounded obnoxious,
but dogs from two blocks away began barking.)

He continued with more instructions. "When I give two whistle blows, you will turn left. Three, and you will turn right. And you will march in perfect step to the drummers, is that clear?"

"When do we play?" Sammy yelled.

"When I blow the one long whistle, you are to raise your instruments to your mouth. Then, when I deliver four short whistles, you will begin playing." (It was more math than I could handle, but Lisa seemed to understand.)

"All right." Billy pointed to the drum section, took another deep breath, and

TWEEEEEEET . . .
TWEET-*TWEET*-TWEET-TWEET

By measuring the length of each of her steps and listening to the band members around her, Lisa was doing really well.

After several steps she heard *TWEET! TWEET!* and, with the rest of the band, she turned left.

After several more steps she heard *TWEET! TWEET! TWEET!* and turned right.

Yes, it was quite a feat, and Lisa couldn't be prouder. Finally, came another

TWEEEEEEET . . .
TWEET-*TWEET*-TWEET-TWEET

and the band began to

play. The drummers drummed, the trumpeters trumpeted, and the saxophonists saxophoned. Everyone played great.

Well, almost everyone. Then there was Lisa:

Waugh-**WAAAAUGH-WOOOOM**...

(Remember those barking dogs? Now add howling cats.)

"Whoa! Whoa!" Billy waved his arms for the band to stop. But Lisa, not seeing Billy, just kept playing with all her heart.

Waugh-**WAAAAUGH-WOOOOM**...
Waugh-**WAAAAUGH-WOOOOM**...

(Now throw in a few screaming babies.)

"HALT!" Billy shouted. "LISA MULLIGAN, I ORDER YOU TO STOP THIS INSTANT!"

Lisa slowed to a stop (although the barking, howling, and screaming continued).

"YOU CALL THAT MUSIC?" he yelled.

Lisa was speechless.

Sadly, Billy wasn't. "GET OFF MY FIELD!" he shouted. "GO BACK TO THE BAND ROOM!"

It was hard to tell if Lisa was more angry, embarrassed, or brokenhearted. Regardless, she now understood that her chances of making the marching band were over. She found her way back to the band room, unable to hide the tears filling her eyes.

Dad had said that all things were supposed to work together for good if she loved God and that loving God meant obeying Him. Well, Dad was wrong. There was no way *this* could work together for anyone's good!

Or so she thought.

19
And Over in the Middle School . . .

CHEERLEADING TRYOUTS were held onstage in the auditorium. And since Chloe would be involved, she asked Coach Buffton if Petey McNurdy from the school's television-production club could videotape it.

"I suppose," Coach said.

"And backstage, too?" Chloe asked.

"Why?" Coach said.

"Because the more of me I see on camera, the happier I am. And the happier I am, the happier Mommy will be. And you know how she loves contributing to your sports programs . . . *if* she's happy."

Coach gave a heavy sigh. "If that makes you happy, sure."

(As I said, Coach Buffton was no fan of Chloe's, but she was a big fan of Mommy's money.)

So as the rest of the middle school took their seats, getting ready for the performance, Chloe was backstage putting on a performance of her own for Petey.

"Oh!" she cried out. "My foot! My foot!"

All her wannabes crowded around her and cried, "Your foot! Your foot! What happened?"

Chloe waited for Petey to bring his camera in for a nice close-up. Then, flipping her perfect hair to the side, she cried, "I think I sprained it." With a pathetic whimper she added, "How will I ever do my cheer now?"

Of course, the wannabes replied: "Oh, no! Poor thing! How will you ever do your cheer now?"

But Chloe had an idea . . .

"Jessica?" she called. "Oh, dear, sweet Jessica?"

Jessica looked up from wrapping her ankle.

With plenty of whimpering for Petey (and the camera), Chloe limped toward her. "I think I sprained my ankle. Just like you."

"Sorry to hear that," Jessica said. And she was (a little). "It can really hurt."

"But it's not stopping *you* from going on," Chloe said.

"As long as I keep it wrapped with this bandage, I'll be okay," Jessica said.

"Oh." Chloe gave a loud sniff. "Do you think maybe I could . . ." She threw in a whimper to make her point. "Do you think I could borrow that wrap?"

"You want to borrow this bandage?" Jessica asked.

Chloe nodded. "I'm going on first. You can go on last. That'll give me plenty of time to finish, race back here, and give it to you so you can wrap your own ankle."

Jessica frowned. She had every reason for not wanting to help. Every reason except that part in the Bible about doing good and loving your enemies. She looked at Chloe, who was not only whimpering and sniffing, but getting her bottom lip to tremble at the same time. Chloe was good at acting, that was for sure. Very good.

"*Please,* Jessica . . ."

Jessica looked back at the wrap on her ankle. Of course she was suspicious. After all, it was Chloe Richardson. But she knew how bad a sprain could hurt and Chloe *had* promised to bring it right back . . .

"*Pleeeeease . . .*" Now tears were streaming down Chloe's face. (I told you she was good.)

"Well, okay," Jessica said. She started unwrapping her ankle. "But you'll bring it back just as soon as you're done, right?"

"Of course."

Reluctantly Jessica handed her the bandage.

Chloe grabbed it and hobbled off, her limp worse than ever. Except . . .

"Chloe?" Jessica called. "Weren't you limping with the other foot?"

"Oh, right," Chloe said, and switched limps. "Thanks."

If Jessica was a little suspicious before, she was a lot suspicious now.

And, sadly, her suspicions proved true. Because when Coach Buffton announced Chloe's name and Chloe went on stage, she was missing not only her limp but also the bandage.

Jessica frowned as Chloe took her place and began:

"Go, go! Get 'em, get 'em!
Bam! Bam!
Go, go! Get 'em, get 'em!
GoooOOOOO ... CLAMS!"

It was perfect in every way (which was no surprise, considering Chloe's private trainer).

But when she finished, Chloe didn't run backstage to return the bandage as she had promised. Instead, she joined her friends in the audience. So as the other contestants did their cheers, Jessica had to limp into the auditorium to find her.

It seemed to take forever until she finally spotted her. "Chloe!" she shouted. "Chloe!"

Chloe turned from her group of admirers.

"Where is it?" Jessica asked.

"Where's what?"

"My ankle wrap?"

"Ankle wrap?"

"Chloe, I can't go on without it," Jessica said.

"You lost your ankle wrap?"

"I didn't lose it, I loaned it to—"

"Oh, you poor thing. How will you ever do your routine?"

Before Jessica could answer, Coach Buffton's voice boomed through the speakers. "Next up: Jessica Mulligan."

"That's you," Chloe said.

"You have it," Jessica said. "Hand it over!"

"Why would I have it?"

"For your ankle!"

"*My* ankle." Chloe laughed, showing her foot. "There's nothing wrong with my ankle."

Coach Buffton repeated: "Jessica Mulligan."

"Chloe . . ."

Chloe batted her eyes in innocence.

Coach called again. "Jessica Mulligan."

"Better hurry." Chloe smiled her every-tooth-in-place smile before turning back to her friends.

With no alternative, Jessica turned, limped through the audience, and hobbled up onto the stage—all the time trying to hide her pain. When she took her place, she gritted her teeth.

"Ready?" Coach Buffton asked.

Jessica nodded. She took a breath and, with a quiet prayer, finally began:

"Go, go! Get 'em, get 'em!

Bam! B—ahHHHHHHH ..."

The pain was so bad she tumbled onto the stage, unable to finish.

Of course people (mostly Chloe's friends) laughed and cheered. But Coach Buffton immediately ran onto the stage.

Helping Jess to her feet, she asked, "Are you all right? Are you okay?"

Jess nodded, but of course she wasn't okay. Not by a long shot.

Over the laughter she heard Chloe shouting, "Poor thing! Must be the Mulligan curse!"

More laughter.

Jessica's face was on fire with embarrassment as Coach helped her limp off the stage. Somewhere in the back of her mind, she was already thinking how wrong Dad was about everything working together for good. Seriously? Jess shook her head. Absolutely not. No way. And it only grew worse when the laughter suddenly turned to screams.

She spun around just in time to see a herd of gazelles leaping over the seats toward the stage. They couldn't run down the aisle because Howdy and Doody filled it. They were the park's two growling ostriches. (Yes, that's right, ostriches can growl; I told you these books were educational.)

By the way, you'd growl too . . . if you were being chased by Bippo, the baby hippo.

20
Curse on the Loose

SO . . . ALL THE STUDENTS RAN out of the auditorium screaming:

"I'LL BE EATEN ALIVE!"
"WHO KNEW OSTRICHES GROWLED!"
(I'm glad somebody was paying attention.)

"WILL MY HOMEWORK BE DUE IN HEAVEN?"

Then, of course, there was the ever popular:

"IT'S THE MULLIGAN CURSE!"

The teachers tried to settle everyone down. Principal Everpal was the best example. She was cool, calm, and collected as she stood in the hallway quietly explaining, "Children, there is no need to panic. Treat the animals with caution and respect, and they will not harm you."

"What about the bats?" Bradley Bartson shouted.

"Please, Bradley, I see no bats."

"That's because they're landing in your hair."

"Don't be ridiculous," she said, reaching up to her head. "There are . . . BATS LANDING IN MY HAIR!" (So much for cool, calm, and collected.)

And it was no different in Stephie's elementary school . . . where Waldo, the park's one and only walrus, was making a special guest appearance. The good news was he never made it inside the school. The bad news was he didn't have to since little Harry Sniffleton's class was on the first floor.

It was little Harry's day for show-and-tell. In the middle of coughing, sniffling, and wiping his nose with the back of his hand (Harry has major problems with allergies . . . *and* personal hygiene), he was proudly showing off his prize queen angelfish,

> . . . and since the best way to show off the fish's beautiful blues, greens, and golds was to put it in the sunlight
>
> . . . and since the best sunlight came through the classroom's open window
>
> . . . and since he set it on the windowsill . . .

> (Well, you probably get the picture.)

Addressing the class, he said, "The angelfish is, *cough-cough,* found mostly in South America; places like, *sniff-sniff,* the Amazon River. But we bought this fish at the pet shop for $299.99, *cough-cough, sniff-sniff.*" (Will somebody please get this kid a tissue before he—*SNIFFFFFFFFF, wipe-wipe*—oh, never mind.) "Angelfish prefer warm water with temperatures between 78 and 84 degrees and—"

Suddenly the class screamed. It was hard for Harry to tell which was louder, the class screaming in front of him or the

SLURP . . .
gulp-ing

behind him.

Either way, when he turned, he saw that his fishbowl was empty. And just beyond it, Waldo was waddling off, not exactly full, but less hungry than

BURP!

he was before.

But that was nothing compared to the tons of problems Lisa's high school faced. Actually, to be exact, three and a half tons—which just happens to be the average weight of female elephants. (Make sure you know this to impress your friends.)

Lisa was in the band room wiping the tears from her eyes as she packed up her trombone. She first suspected something was wrong when the entire marching band ran in. And she suspected it might have to do with an elephant when they kept screaming, "It's an elephant! It's an elephant!"

"What?" she cried.

Sammy Dimberg shouted, "There's a wild elephant on the football field!"

"Are you sure?" she asked.

"Kinda hard to miss a wild elephant!" Sammy said.

Of course Lisa knew it couldn't be wild. There aren't that many wild elephants roaming around the city. In fact, the last time she counted, there was a grand total of zero.

So if it wasn't wild, it had to be . . .

"Buttercup!" she gasped.

"Who?" Sammy said.

"Is she hurt?" Lisa asked. "Nobody hurt her, did they?"

"We were too busy running for our lives," Sammy said. "Except . . ."

"Except what?"

"You know how Billy loves to be in control."

Lisa nodded.

"Well, when the elephant refused to get off the field, he started shouting and yelling at it."

"But the elephant didn't charge, did she?" Lisa asked. "Buttercup wouldn't hurt a fly."

"No, she didn't charge Billy, but Billy kind of . . ."

"What?!" Lisa asked, growing more and more concerned. "Billy kind of what?"

"He kind of ran at the elephant, swinging his giant baton. And that kind of bothered the elephant, so she kind of—"

Lisa didn't stick around for the rest of the story. She raced out of the band room.

None of this made sense. What was Buttercup doing at the school? Why had Billy attacked her? And why was Lisa asking these crazy questions when she already knew the answer had to do with the

CURSE ... urse ... urse ...

21

A Private Performance

BY THE TIME LISA REACHED the football field, the SWAT team was already climbing out of their van. They were old pals from when Freda, one of our leopards, had Nick trapped on the balcony of a hotel and Lisa had to try to calm Freda down.

"Hi there, Lisa," one called out.

"Good seeing you again, Lisa," another shouted.

"Sorry we have to shoot your elephant," another one said.

Lisa froze in her tracks. "Sorry you have to WHAT? You can't shoot Buttercup!" she cried.

"Hopefully not," the commander said. "That's why Mel, our sharpshooter, has the tranquilizer gun. If he can hit her, we'll put her to sleep like we tried with your leopard."

"What exactly did Buttercup do?" Lisa asked.

The commander motioned to the top of the bleachers where Buttercup had Billy trapped. "See for yourself," he said.

Of course, Lisa couldn't "see for herself" (being blind has that effect on people), but she could hear Billy shouting and pictured him swinging his giant baton back and forth. "Get back, you stupid animal!" he cried. "Get back!"

And she could hear Buttercup

CRY-ing
GRUNT-ing

and

TRUMPET-ing

in anger.

Lisa turned to the commander. "Please," she begged, "let me talk to her."

"We hoped you would," he said. "But I'm positioning Mel and spreading the rest of my men out to get a clean shot should she attack you."

"She won't attack me," Lisa said as she headed for the bleachers—while adding, under her breath, "I hope."

Billy saw her and yelled, "Hey, Mulligan, tell your stupid animal to leave me alone!"

"Maybe if you stopped yelling at and threatening her!"

"Tell her to stop!" Billy said as he took a couple more swings at Buttercup. "BACK, YOU STUPID CRITTER! BACK!"

Buttercup answered by shaking her head and throwing in some more

CRY-ing

GRUNT-ing

and

TRUMPET-ing

"Billy, stop!" Lisa cried.

"Tell *her* to stop! She started it!"

Lisa had hoped Billy would be more mature than the elephant. But realizing she was wrong, she called to Buttercup, "Hey, girl. Hey, Buttercup. Hey, girl, it's me."

The elephant turned at the sound of her voice.

"It's okay, girl," Lisa said, "he's not going to hurt you."

Buttercup shook her head and snorted.

"I get it," Lisa said. "We all feel that way about him."

"I heard that!" Billy shouted.

When Lisa got close, she reached up and patted Buttercup's side. "Good girl. You're a good girl, aren't you?"

But Billy was still playing his blame game. "She started it, not me!" he yelled.

"If I were you, I'd climb down from there," Lisa said. "While I'm distracting her, get down as fast as you can."

Even though it wasn't his idea, it seemed a good one, and he quickly scrambled down the bleachers past Buttercup—but not before hitting her on the head with his metal baton. (As the least mature of the two, he had no choice.)

"HAAH!" he shouted. "You stupid animal!"

Unfortunately, Buttercup wasn't the one acting stupid.

Unfortunatlier (there's that word again), she gave a loud

B E L L O W

and turned and charged after him.

Lisa shouted, "Buttercup!"

But the elephant didn't stop.

Billy ran for cover under the bleachers.

Buttercup followed. Once she arrived, she began ramming into the bleachers, trying to reach him.

"Shoot her!" Billy shouted. "Somebody shoot her!"

"Mel?" the commander called to his sharpshooter with the tranquilizer gun.

"I can't get a clear shot!" Mel cried.

Meanwhile, Buttercup kept hitting the bleachers, bending and breaking them as she got closer and closer to Billy.

"Shoot her!" Billy screamed. "What are you waiting for?"

"Take your positions," the SWAT leader called to his men.

"Buttercup!" Lisa cried. "Stop!"

But Buttercup wasn't stopping. The fact that Billy was able to reach through and land a few hits with his baton didn't help. In fact, it made her all the more angry, and she smashed more of the bleachers.

"Help me!" Billy screamed.

"Prepare to fire!" the commander shouted to his men.

"NO!" Lisa cried. "She doesn't understand!"

"Stupid animal!" Billy shouted, and hit her again. "HAAH!"

"Billy!" Lisa yelled as Buttercup continued

CRY-ing
GRUNT-ing

and

TRUMPET-ing

"Buttercup!"

"Aim!" the commander shouted.

"Shoot her! SHOOT HER!"

"NOOO!"

And then, just when it looked like Billy would get his way,

WOOOOR . . . waaaugh waaaugh
BRAAUGH . . .

Lisa raised her head. Was it possible? Was there somebody playing the trombone even worse than her?

"Hey, Lisa?"

Recognizing his voice, she shouted, "Nick!"

"How do you work this thing?" he yelled.

"What are you doing?" she cried.

"Dad called. Said all the animals have escaped."

"That's terrible, but—"

"Someone saw Buttercup out here, and I figured you might need a hand." Turning to the SWAT commander, he shouted, "Hold your fire, guys! We've got a secret weapon here." As he joined Lisa, he handed her the trombone.

Lisa frowned. "What am I supposed to—"

"Play it," he said.

"Will somebody shoot this thing?" Billy cried.

Nick yelled, "Chill, Bill!" Then turning back to Lisa, he repeated, "Play it. Play like Buttercup's life depended on it."

Lisa understood. She raised the trombone to her lips.

Billy screamed, "I'm about to die! Doesn't anybody—"

And she started to

Waugh-*WAAAA UG H*-wOOOOM . . .

"What are you doing!" Billy cried.

Nick shouted, "She's saving your life!"

Waugh-WAAAAUGH-WOOOOM . . .

Slowly Buttercup turned from Billy toward Lisa. Then, tilting back her head, Buttercup answered with her own

atreee-Waa . . .

Which, of course, Lisa answered back with

Waugh-WAAAAUGH-WOOOOM . . .

To which Buttercup answered

atreee-Waa . . .

"Keep it up!" Nick shouted. "You're as bad as ever." Then to Billy he yelled, "If I were you, I'd get out of there while the getting's good."

Billy didn't have to be told twice. He scrambled out from the bleachers and ran as fast as he could while Lisa and Buttercup continued their

Waugh-WAAAAUGH-WOOOOM-ing

and

atreee-Waa-ing.

22
Halftime Huddle

AND OUR ANIMALS WEREN'T JUST in the schools. The whole town was going crazy with them. Which meant our phone was ringing off the hook:

"Excuse me, Mr. Mulligan, but your moose is eating my petunias."

"We'll get right on it!"

"Excuse me, Mrs. Mulligan, but your tortoise is in my bathtub."

"We'll send someone out!"

"Excuse me, but your orangutan is in my car."

"I'll be right—What? In your car?" Dad asked. "Where?"

"Main Street."

"What part of Main Street?"

"All of it."

"All of it?"

"I left the car running and dashed into the market to buy some milk."

"And?"

"While I was in there, it got into my car, climbed behind the wheel, and . . ."

Dad groaned, "You don't mean . . ."

"That's right. He's driving up and down Main Street as we speak."

The good news was they let all us Mulligans out of school to come home and help. Except me. You have to be in school to be let out of school. Not that I haven't tried. But I usually get caught the first day. Not because I refuse to take off my fur coat (which I've mentioned I'm kind of attached to) but because all those pencils are just too tasty to pass up.

So we all gathered in the family room and waited for Dad to give out assignments.

"I just don't understand," Jessica said. "Why is all this happening to us?"

"I told you," Hector whispered, "it's the curse."

"I thought it was ghosts," Stephie said.

Hector nodded. "Probably both."

"Guys," Dad said. "How many times do we have to tell you, there are no such things as curses and ghosts."

"So what *is* happening?" Janelle asked.

Dad shook his head. "I don't know. But who or whatever it is, we can still beat it."

"That's right," Nick said. "Nothing can stop us because we're the magnificent Mulligans!"

Normally there would be cheers or some high fives. But by now we all had our doubts.

"You *are* magnificent," Mom said. "But remember, we've got something even better."

"What's that?" Hector asked.

"God," little Julie chirped.

Mom smiled. "That's right. And we've got prayer."

Dad nodded and said, "She's got a good point."

"So why don't we do it?" Stephie asked.

"You mean, pray?" Jessica said. "Here? Now?"

"Here and now is when we need it," Mom said. "Anybody feeling like giving it a shot?"

Immediately little Julie's hand shot up. "Me! Me! Can I?"

The rest of us should have been just as excited, but we were either too cool or thought we were too grown up.

But not Julie. Right then she was the coolest and most grown up of the bunch. Without a word, she reached out and grabbed Jessica's hand on her right and Janelle's on her left. We took her cue and did the same—everyone reaching out until we were all holding hands. And then we bowed our heads.

"Dear God . . ." she said. "We sure like You and . . ." She scrunched up her forehead, trying to think of something else. "And please fix all this. Amen."

I suppose her prayer could have been longer, but if you ask me, she covered it all. Everybody else thought so, too, because we all said, "Amen" and "OO-oo AH-ah EE-ee."

"Okay." Dad clapped his hands. "Let's gather around the table and make some plans. We'll go out in pairs, each of us covering a specific area of the town."

"Do you think we'll be done in time?" Nick asked.

Dad turned to him. "In time for . . . ?"

"Your big debate tonight."

Dad shook his head. "I'm canceling tonight's debate. In fact, I'm pulling out of the election."

"You're quitting?" Lisa said. "You're letting Mayor Jowls win?"

"Our animals are terrorizing the town," Dad said. "The election is tomorrow. What the mayor says is true. If I can't run an animal park, how can I run a town?"

"But, Dad—" Nick argued.

"Sorry, Son. I'm canceling tonight's debate and conceding tomorrow's election. I have no choice."

"Actually . . ." Lisa said, "that's not true."

We turned to her.

"You do have one other choice," she said.

Dad frowned.

She continued. "You can trust God."

"Lisa, I've—"

"Just like I had to trust Him today when I tried out for the marching band."

"But you didn't make it," Jessica said.

Nick agreed. "But she did something greater."

Lisa nodded. "I saved Buttercup's life—which is a lot more important."

"And," Nick added, "she may have saved Billy Egobrat."

"Yeah," Lisa sighed. "I suppose him, too."

Before Dad could respond, Nick asked him, "How's that Bible verse go again? 'For those who love God all things work together for good.'"

"That's right," Janelle said. "Not *some* things—"

Lisa added, "Not *most* things. But . . ." She waited for Dad to answer.

He chuckled quietly and finally said, "*All* things."

"That's right," Nick said.

Still smiling, Dad shook his head, a little embarrassed and a lot pleased. "You guys . . ."

Mom grinned. "Looks like they had a pretty good teacher."

Dad gave his eyes a quick swipe then cleared his throat. "Okay, then." He motioned us toward the table. "Let's not stand around. We've got plenty to do!"

This time we *did* cheer and high-five. Because there's one thing you can say about us Mulligans: When the chips are down, we're always there for each other.

(Unless those chips are potato—in which case it's every chimp for herself!)

23
The Debate

THE GOOD NEWS IS, we got most of the animals back home before the debate. The bad news is, MOST is not the same as ALL. Even as we headed into the auditorium to watch Dad, we were getting last-minute calls. Little things like:

"Help! Help! There's a giant cobra climbing up our birdcage and—"

tweet-tweet
gulp
BURP

"—never mind."

"Help! Help! There's a giant gorilla on my skateboard and—"

gurrrr . . .
thud
whimper-whimper-whimper

"—never mind."

"Help! Help! There's a giant piranha in our toilet and—"

FLUSH . . .
glug-glug-glug

"—never mind."

Of course I ran into my usual problems when I tried entering the auditorium with the rest of the family.

"Sorry," the usher said, "no animals."

But Stephie and I were used to this type of prejudice. Within minutes we returned with my favorite disguise— lying in a baby carriage, wearing a baby bonnet and sucking a pacifier.

Of course the usher still stopped us. But when he looked down at my hairy face, he let out a gasp. "Oh, my, I'm so sorry!"

"Is there a problem?" Stephie asked.

"Uh, no, miss," the usher said. He tried to smile. "What um, er, a cute baby you have!" (It almost sounded like a lie. Then again, just because he was prejudiced didn't mean he couldn't recognize great beauty.)

Soon we were all in the auditorium along with a live audience and TV cameras. Everyone was watching Dad and Mayor Jowls on stage debating.

I'll spare you all the boring stuff about taxes, and schools, and taxes, and—did I mention taxes?

But I won't spare you the part where Mayor Jowls started saying mean things about Dad. First he called him a crook. Then a liar. Then a stupid, crooked liar.

"Do you honestly think you're smarter than me," the mayor said, "just because you run some wild-animal park?"

Of course Dad didn't like the name-calling. But instead of saying mean stuff back, he tried to be respectful. "I'm sorry you feel that way, Mr. Mayor, but please understand, I'm not questioning your intelligence. In fact, I think you've made some very smart choices for our city."

"Oh, yeah?" the mayor yelled back. "Well, that shows how little you know, because I—" He came to a stop when he realized that Dad had actually complimented him.

The audience was also confused and started to murmur. This isn't what they came to hear.

But Dad continued. "And I'm sure there's a lot I can learn from you regarding—"

"That's another lie!" the mayor shouted. "And I resent the fact that . . . wait, what?"

"It's true," Dad said. "You have done a lot of good."

The mayor looked even more confused. So did the audience.

The cameras moved in for a close-up as Dad continued. "But there are some issues I think I would approach differently."

Unable to stand the politeness, the mayor fired back.

"That's the problem with you, Mulligan. You don't have time to think! Not with that big family and all those animals."

"Mr. Mayor." Dad's voice grew firmer. "With all due respect, my family is—"

The mayor interrupted. "You know nothing about running a city!"

"You've made that point already, but what you're missing—"

"You can't even run an animal park!"

"Mr. Mayor—"

"How many of those animals have escaped this week?"

"Actually, quite a few. And I'm trying to get to the bottom of what happened. But that's really not the—"

"And how many of them have gotten loose *today*?" Before Dad could answer, the mayor shouted, "All of them! And they're running all over my town, terrorizing my people."

"We've managed to collect most of—"

"You're not smart, Mulligan. You're stupid! Just like the animals in your park." Looking into the TV camera, he continued shouting. "And anybody stupid enough to vote for you . . . well, I pity them because they're just plain . . . well, stupid!"

The mayor turned to the audience. He was pleased with his performance. And by the way many of them began clapping, they were pleased too. This was the fight they wanted to see . . . not some nice guy giving thoughtful answers.

It was clear that Dad was losing.

But instead of worrying, Mom kept looking to Dad up on the stage like she was really proud.

Stephie leaned over to her and whispered, "What's wrong with Daddy? Why isn't he being mean like Mayor Jowls?"

Still smiling, Mom answered, "He's doing it God's way."

"He's what?"

Mom whispered back, "The Bible says to stand for truth but not to return evil for evil."

Stephie sat back in her seat, frowning.

When the applause died down, the mayor looked over to Dad and sneered, "So what do you have to say for yourself, Mulligan?"

Dad took a deep breath and, still keeping calm, he answered. "Some of what you've said is true. We don't understand yet how the animals have escaped. But much of what you said is *not* true. So, getting back to the issues of this election—"

BARK BARK BARK

Dad stopped at the interruption. He tried again. "I believe what our city needs is a fresh perspective on how—"

BARK BARK BARK

He stopped again. And for good reason. Off to the left, Larry, Moe, and Curly, the three missing seals, were slipping and sliding across the stage. We watched in stunned silence as they waddled right in front of Dad and the mayor.

At first everyone gasped. Then they all laughed . . . most of all, Mayor Jowls.

Dad tried to smile. But it was obvious to everybody, even Mom, that he had just lost the debate . . . and most likely the election.

24
And the Winner Is . . .

THE FOLLOWING MORNING Billy Egobrat posted the sign announcing who made the marching band. And if Lisa was expecting some happily-ever-after fairy-tale ending, she was wrong. Billy hated fairy tales. Then again, maybe it was his prejudice against blind people—or bad trombone playing.

Of course Lisa felt bad. But one thing you could say about Lisa Mulligan: She was no quitter. Every time she got knocked down, she got back up, all the stronger. Or as Grandpa Mulligan once told her, "Every time the devil kicks you in the rear, it just lifts you closer to heaven." The bottom line? She'd be working harder, practicing longer . . . and we'd be buying earplugs. By this time next year she'd be better than good, she'd be the best. And who knows, with Billy Egobrat graduating and going off to college, she might even try out for drum major—a relief for all of us since drum majors don't play instruments.

What was it Dad said about God wanting to give us a better good than the good we may think we want? Maybe it was true. I mean, let's face it: Saving an elephant and a person's life (even if it was Billy Egobrat's) was a thousand times better than making some marching band. And maybe by this time next year she might have it all.

Meanwhile, over in the middle school . . .

Everyone was in the lunchroom eating. Or in Chloe's case, holding court with all her wannabes. "I can hardly wait for the announcement," she said to her table of clones. "I just hope I make it."

"Oh, you will," they answered. "For sure," they said. "Absolutely," they replied. "You'll be the captain," her fan club president said.

Chloe flipped her hair to the side. "Who, me?" She tried to be modest, but some things are impossible, even for the great Chloe Richardson. "I'm not so sure," she said.

Flipping their hair to the side, the clones all answered, "Oh, you will." "For sure." "Absolutely."

Jessica ate nearby at another table. As far as she was concerned, things had definitely not worked together for good.

But looking at her sandwich, she was at least grateful for not getting six pieces of bread covered in mustard and mayo.

"Attention. May I have your attention?"

Everyone continued talking, ignoring Coach Buffton, who appeared on the big-screen TV at the front of the cafeteria.

"SILENCE!"

The room fell silent. (Coach Buffton was used to getting her way.) She continued, "We have the votes for this year's cheerleaders. Everyone did a great job. But here are the winners."

Jessica slumped down into her chair.

Coach Buffton began reading off the names. "Heather Hankerson, Moonglow Lamplighter, Mitch Machoman . . ." There were a dozen names, and after each one, the kids clapped, cheered, and—in Mitch's case—grunted . . . as Jessica scooted further and further down into her seat.

"And finally," Coach said, "for the last position, we have a tie. It's between Chloe Richardson and . . . Jessica Mulligan."

If there was silence before, it was deafening now. Well, except at Chloe Richardson's table. "What?!" Chloe cried. "I never lose!"

"What?!" her clones cried. "She never loses!"

The rest of the cafeteria murmured in agreement. This was obviously a new concept for all of them.

Coach Buffton continued, "To represent our school, a cheerleader must not only be a skilled athlete but work together as a team player."

"I'm all that!" Chloe cried.

"She's all that!" her clones cried.

Coach continued, "In just a moment we'll be voting between the two, but first I want you to see the video Peter McNurdy made during yesterday's tryouts."

The screen went blank and then . . .

> *Chloe appeared backstage, limping toward Jessica. "Oh, dear, sweet Jessica. I think I sprained my ankle. Just like you."*
>
> *"Sorry to hear that," Jessica said. "It can really hurt."*
>
> *"But it's not stopping you from going on," Chloe said.*
>
> *"As long as I keep it wrapped with this bandage, I'll be okay," Jessica said.*
>
> *"Oh. Do you think I could borrow that wrap?"*
>
> *"You want to borrow this bandage?" Jessica asked.*
>
> *Chloe nodded. "I'm going on first. You can go on last. That'll give me plenty of time to finish, race back here, and give it to you so you can wrap your own ankle." By now Chloe was sniffing and getting her bottom lip to tremble. "Please, Jessica. Pleeeeease . . ."*
>
> *Jessica hesitated, then finally said, "Well, okay." She started unwrapping her ankle. "But you'll bring it back just as soon as you're done, right?"*
>
> *"Of course."*

The video clip ended. Coach Buffton reappeared on the screen, saying, "Then, after her stellar performance, Peter managed to capture this."

The video resumed:

Jessica was limping toward Chloe, calling her name.

Chloe turned from her group of admirers.

"Where is it?" Jessica demanded.

"Where's what?"

"My ankle wrap?"

"Ankle wrap?"

"Chloe, I can't go on without it."

"You lost your ankle wrap?"

"I didn't lose it, I loaned it to—"

"Oh, you poor thing. How will you ever do your routine?"

"You have it!" Jessica said. "Hand it over!"

"Why would I have it?"

"For your ankle!"

"My ankle." Chloe laughed, showing her foot. "There's nothing wrong with my ankle."

The scene froze on screen as Coach Buffton entered the cafeteria. "So," she said, "my question to you is, *Who do you really want to represent our school?* Chloe Richardson—"

Chloe jumped to her feet. "That's all fake. I'd never do anything like that—not if I knew it was going to be taped!"

Coach finished, "—or Jessica Mulligan?"

Jessica sat, too stunned to say anything.

Not that she could be heard over Chloe's screaming, "It was all photoshopped. Special effects. You know, like the movies!"

"Chloe?" Coach said.

But Chloe didn't hear. "Petey McNurdy, my mother is going to call your mother and—"

"CHLOE RICHARDSON!" Coach Buffton didn't exactly roar, but it was close enough for Chloe to melt back into her seat. Turning to the rest of the cafeteria, Coach asked, "So who will it be? Who do you want as a cheerleader? Chloe Richardson?"

All the hands at Chloe's table shot up—both left and right.

"Okay," Coach said. "And how many of you would rather have Jessica Mulligan represent us?"

Slowly, one by one, hands began to rise across the room.

"What?" Chloe cried. "Stop that!"

"What?" her clones cried. "Stop that!"

And more hands rose.

"Don't you know who I am?" Chloe demanded.

"Don't you know who she is?" her wannabes demanded.

But this time, nobody cared.

Jessica looked around the room absolutely speechless. It took all her strength not to cry, but soon every hand had raised. Then someone began to clap. And then another, and another. It was hopeless. Try as she might, tears slipped from Jessica's eyes and began streaming down her face. Soon, everyone in the room was applauding . . . so loud you could no longer hear the hysterical shouts of Chloe and her clones.

25
Wrapping Up

FOR THOSE OF YOU KEEPING SCORE, Dad lost the election by one gazillion, three hundred seventy thousand votes (or something like that) to two. I wanted to join Mom and Dad to make it three votes, but they said I was too young. (And too . . . nonhuman.)

And as far as the other score, the one where all things work together for good for those who love God? The way I see it, it was a tie:

GOD WINS: 2 points
- Jessica made the cheerleading squad.
- Lisa saved Buttercup (and Billy Egobrat).

GOD LOSES: 2 points
- Dad lost the election.
- We're still under the curse.

At least that was the score until tonight . . .

We were all sitting around watching Mayor Jowls give his victory speech on TV (how they could squeeze that big man into that flat screen was amazing). As you can imagine, there was plenty of food being thrown at the screen . . . until Mom made me leave the room.

I was just going when someone knocked on the door. I walked over to open it. To my surprise, there stood Officer Tippet. Beside him was Madame Claire, the fortune teller from the carnival.

"May we come in?" he asked.

"OO-oo AH-ah EE-ee," I said, and motioned them inside.

The moment they entered, Nick's face brightened. "All right!" he said. "You've come to sell us those chicken feathers!"

"Sorry, folks," Officer Tippet said. "No chicken feathers on sale tonight."

"But . . ." Hector frowned. "How do we get rid of the curse?"

"There is no curse," the officer said.

Remembering her manners, Mom motioned to the sofa. "Please, won't you have a seat?"

"Thank you," they said.

Once they got settled, Dad asked, "So . . . what's this all about?"

Officer Tippet motioned to the TV. "Would you mind turning that down?"

"With pleasure," Lisa said. She hit the mute button. The mayor continued talking but without saying anything . . . which, come to think of it, was what he always did.

Turning to Madame Claire, Officer Tippet asked, "Do you want to tell them, or should I?"

"Thank you, Officer," she said, "but I believe I should."

"Wait a minute," Janelle said, "what happened to your accent?"

Madame Claire shook her head. "That's merely for entertainment, dear. It's how I make my living."

"So . . ." Nick asked, "the chicken feathers are definitely out?"

Madame Claire smiled sadly. "There is no curse. There never has been."

"But . . ." Hector said.

Madame Claire continued. "Your mayor promised our company a handsome sum of money to make those in town think your family was cursed. And for those who don't believe in curses, it was to convince them that your father was a bad manager of your park."

"I don't get it," Stephie said.

Madame Claire explained. "We used some of our trucks to steal your animals and move them around your town."

"That was . . . *you*?" Jessica asked. "All of it?"

Madame Claire nodded. "I am afraid so."

Officer Tippet stepped in. "And they would have gotten

away with it, too, except . . ." He looked back to the woman, waiting for her to answer.

She turned to Dad. "I saw the debate last night. Your answers were so respectful and so honest, I couldn't let the mayor get away with his scheme."

Officer Tippet added, "That, plus the fact he never paid you."

She shrugged. "There is that."

"So . . ." Lisa asked, "this was all so the mayor could win the election?"

"That's right," Officer Tippet said.

"What a jerk," Nick grumbled.

"Nick," Dad warned.

"Sorry," Nick said. "But the guy still won. He's still our mayor."

"Well, not exactly." Officer Tippet nodded to the television, where two of his officers were grabbing Mayor Jowls by the arms. Jowls squirmed, but he was no match for them as they escorted him off the platform. The camera followed them down the aisle and into the parking lot toward a waiting police car.

"You're arresting the mayor?" Mom exclaimed.

Officer Tippet nodded. "He's broken several laws with this scheme."

We all stared until Jessica finally asked, "But . . . who will be mayor now?"

"That's up to the city council to decide." Officer Tippet looked to Dad with a grin. "But I have a pretty good idea who they'll select."

We all turned to Dad. It looked like he was having a hard time speaking . . . and maybe a harder time swallowing. He reached out to Mom, who was already dabbing her eyes with a tissue.

"All right, Daddy!" Stephie shouted.

The rest of us crowded around him cheering, knuckle bumping, and throwing in a couple

"OO-oo AH-ah EE-ee"-s

The grown-ups said lots more boring stuff—like how the carnival was going to pay for damages to the animal park and how, with the right lawyer, the carnival's owners would probably not be joining the mayor in his new home away from home—the one with the narrow cot, hard floor, and iron bars.

But none of that mattered to me. I was too busy looking for the TV remote (it had been a good hour since we ate) and reworking the scoreboard in my head. Because things had definitely changed. Now the score was clearly:

GOD WINS: 4 points
GOD LOSES: 0 points

If you ask me, it felt great to be on the winning team. Which, with God, I guess that's always the case . . . since He's used to getting His way. And since He promised that no matter how dark things may get, or how long it may take, He does indeed work all things together for good for those who love Him.

Thoughts and Questions

Chapter 1

1. Sometimes other people can be a little like those crazy mirrors in a carnival fun house—they try to make us think we have big flaws inside us. Have you every been tempted to believe the crazy, fun-house-mirrors stories that the world says about who you are? How did that make you feel?

2. The world's stories about us are not true. When we confess that Jesus is Lord, God sees us through the redemptive work of Jesus—we're as perfect as the Son of God! How can you better recognize and believe what God says about you? (His opinion is the one that really counts!)

3. When we ask God to forgive us, He removes our sins from us "*as far as the east is from the west*" (*Psalm 103:12*). Yes, God continues to guide us and help us make wise decisions so that we can better align with His will and plan for our lives. But as that's

happening, He loves us and is fully on our side. How does this reassure you as you continue to make mistakes and then learn and grow from them?

Chapter 2

1. In the race for mayor, Dad says he isn't going to say mean things about Mayor Jowls, even though the mayor says mean things about him. Consider these comments from Jesus: *"But love your enemies, and do good, and lend, expecting nothing in return, and your reward will be great, and you will be sons of the Most High, for he is kind to the ungrateful and the evil"* (*Luke 6:35*). How does Dad's attitude line up with what Jesus said?
2. What are some areas (and who are some people) in your life that you can apply this truth to?

Chapter 3

1. God makes His position on fortune tellers clear: *"I will cut off sorceries from your hand, and you shall have no more tellers of fortunes"* (*Micah 5:12*). Why do you think God cares about this issue?

Chapter 4

1. How do you think God sees people's fear of ghosts or curses? Even if such things existed, should we

be afraid of them? How do you think God's power compares to the power of the devil?

2. Look at what God says about the power that He gives us: *"Behold, I have given you authority . . . over all the power of the enemy, and nothing shall hurt you"* (*Luke 10:19*). How does knowing this reassure you?

Chapter 5

1. Do we give the devil too much credit when we think every bad thing that happens is his doing? Should we still pray about those things?

Chapter 6

1. Why do you think the Mulligans on the bus thought that the broken bug cage was a result of Madame Claire's "curse"? Is it easy to jump to conclusions based on limited information or a false belief? When has that happened in your life?

Chapter 7

1. As the mixed-up lunches show, things are getting a little crazy for the Mulligan kids and their temptation to believe Madame Claire's "curse" is real. If you were

a friend to one of them, what would you tell them? What would you do for them?

Chapter 8

1. How would you have responded to Mom when she said, "*An eye for an eye and a tooth for a tooth*" (*Matthew 5:38*)?
2. How does Jesus tell us to treat those who treat us poorly? Here's a huge hint: "*Love your enemies and pray for those who persecute you . . .*" (*Matthew 5:44*). How might your life look if you were to treat your "enemies" with love and kindness?

Chapter 9

1. What happened to Jessica may be one of the reasons God tells us not to pay attention to fortune tellers. Have you ever believed so hard that something bad will happen that you may have actually caused it to happen?

Chapter 10

1. Much of this story centers on the Bible's promise in Romans that tells us that God works through all things—even the seemingly very unpleasant ones—for good for those who love Him. In response to this promise, what does Mom say we should do, regardless of whether or not we understand what's going on?

2. Dad says we don't really thank God for the bad stuff, but we thank Him in the middle of it. What's the difference?

Chapter 11

1. The Mulligan kids are really starting to think that Mom and Dad are wrong about ghosts. Have you ever had that happen—believing your parents are wrong, only to discover later that they were right? Can you think of a specific time that happened?

Chapter 12

1. A crocodile in the shower! Things are really looking nasty now. If there are no curses or ghosts, why do bad things keep happening?
2. Do you know people like Chloe Richardson? Instead of counting her as an enemy or disliking her, what would Jesus have Jessica do?

Chapter 13

1. Have you ever met people like Mayor Jowls who always want attention? Does God love them any less than He loves you?
2. Instead of resenting them, maybe we should feel sorry for them. And if we feel sorry for them, what should we do?

Chapter 14

1. Once again we see Nick's pride getting him into trouble. Or as the Bible says, *"Pride goes before destruction, and a haughty spirit before a fall"* (*Proverbs 16:18*). Have you ever seen that happen in other people's lives?
2. Have you seen it happen in your own life? How?

Chapter 15

1. Nick proudly says he's going to stop the curse and capture the ghosts. Whose help is he forgetting to include? How could he be better at getting that help?

Chapter 16

1. Now Nick brings others along on his mission to capture the ghosts. Again, they neglect to rely on God's wisdom and presence. When are some times that you've avoided leaning on God when facing a challenging situation? How you can you be better at seeking that help?

Chapter 17

1. Mom tells Janelle that God never promises us that things will be fair but that Romans 8:28 still applies. What does she mean when she says that our version of *good* isn't as good as God's version?

2. Can you think of a time when God's good was greater than the good you wanted?

Chapter 18

1. "Get off my field!" Billy yells at Lisa. She sure feels defeated. Oftentimes God's greatest victories happen when things look the most hopeless. Can you think of a time that happened in your own life?
2. Have there been times in your life when God didn't immediately fix a problem but waited so He could fix an even bigger one? What happened?

Chapter 19

1. Jessica believed that Chloe needed the ankle wrap. Should Jessica have helped Chloe?
2. Do you think God could have helped Chloe? How?

Chapter 20

1. There's an old expression: "It's always darkest before the dawn." What do you think that means? Can you see the truth of that saying here?
2. Did you notice how quick Lisa was to give the so-called curse the credit and not believe Romans 8:28? Have situations ever happened that caused you to disbelieve the Bible? Explain what happened.

3. Did you wait long enough to see God use those situations for a good greater than the good you thought you wanted?

Chapter 21

1. God can be creative in His solutions. Did you ever think Lisa's bad trombone playing (that Billy can't stand) could actually save Billy's life?
2. Can you think of hard things that actually wind up being good?
3. Do you see how Romans 8:28 finally applies?

Chapter 22

1. Remember how Nick tried to solve the "ghost" problem on his own? How is little Julie's solution different from his?
2. Even after their prayer, Dad is about to quit until the kids remind him of God's promises. Does that necessarily mean Dad will win the election? Why or why not?

Chapter 23

1. Mom tells Stephie that Dad is debating the mayor God's way. How is that?
2. Can you disagree with someone and still honor that person? How?

Chapter 24

1. The Bible tells us to "*count it all joy*" (*James 1:2*) when we hit hard times. Why? Because God will use it to make us "*perfect and complete, lacking in nothing*" (*James 1:4*). Do you see how that can happen with Lisa?

2. What hard times are you going through? Does God want you to count it *all* joy? Do you think it will make you "*perfect and complete, lacking in nothing*"? Why or why not?

3. God has made all things work together for good for Jessica. Sometimes it happens right away or, as in Lisa's case, it may take time. Have you ever been impatient with God and later saw it work out for the best? Are you impatient with something now? What should you do?

Chapter 25

1. Isn't it amazing how God often appears to be losing but always wins at the very end?

2. How did Dad's obedience to God about not returning evil for evil turn everything around?

3. Would it have turned things around if Dad had disobeyed?

4. Do you see how the conditions of both *loving* and *obeying* God are necessary for the promise in Romans 8:28 to apply in your life?

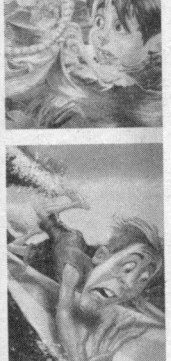

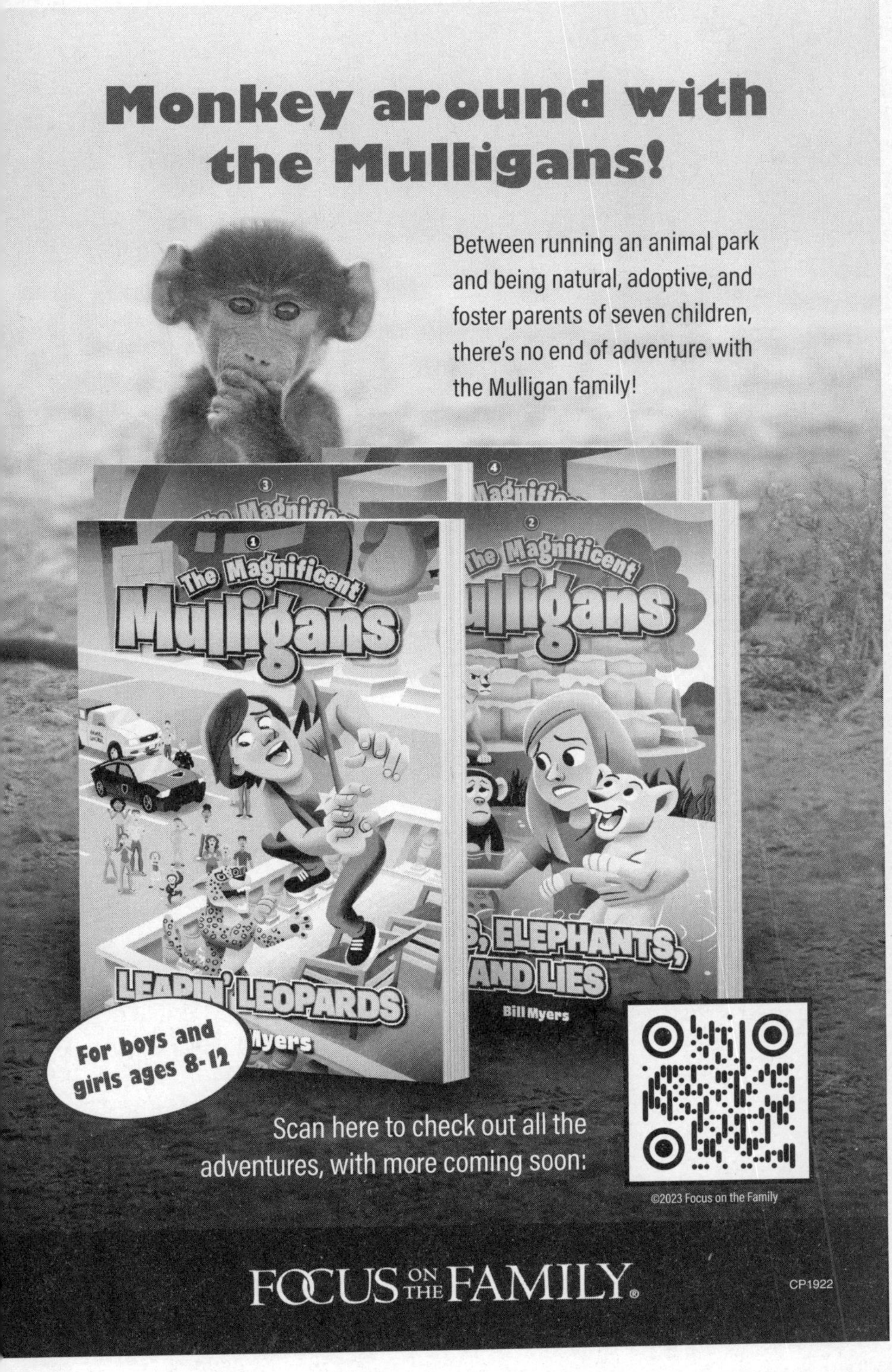
Monkey around with the Mulligans!
Between running an animal park and being natural, adoptive, and foster parents of seven children, there's no end of adventure with the Mulligan family!
The Magnificent Mulligans
Leapin' Leopards
The Magnificent Mulligans
Elephants, and Lies
Bill Myers
For boys and girls ages 8-12
Scan here to check out all the adventures, with more coming soon:
©2023 Focus on the Family
FOCUS ON THE FAMILY®
CP1922

MORE FUN!

Want more cool stories like this? Check out *Focus on the Family's Clubhouse®* Magazine! Each magazine comes with a new comic every month. You'll also get stories from your favorite characters, jokes, puzzles, and more!

Explore the magazine:
FocusOnTheFamily.com/Clubhouse